FALL LIKE LIGHTNING FROM HEAVEN

MARGARET MENDENHALL

FALL LIKE LIGHTNING FROM HEAVEN

TATE PUBLISHING
AND ENTERPRISES, LLC

Published by Tate Publishing & Enterprises, LLC

127 E. Trade Center Terrace | Mustang, Oklahoma 73064 USA
1.888.361.9473 | www.tatepublishing.com

Tate Publishing is committed to excellence in the publishing industry. The company reflects the philosophy established by the founders, based on Psalm 68:11,

"The Lord gave the word and great was the company of those who published it."

Book design copyright © 2012 by Tate Publishing, LLC. All rights reserved.
Cover design by Kate Stearman
Interior design by Blake Brasor

Published in the United States of America
ISBN: 978-1-61777-971-8
Fiction, Christian, Historical
12.1.13

Dedication

This book is dedicated to all the pastors and teachers who have armed themselves with the truth of the authority of the believer and have boldly proclaimed this overcoming message in spite of popular trends and much opposition. This includes my pastor—who just happens to be my husband—that has preached these principles faithfully for thirty-four years.

Acknowledgment

Writing a fiction book of this type required a great deal of encouragement and prayer from many individuals. My thanks to:

My husband, Charlie, who urged me to branch out into fiction—he insists I have too vivid an imagination to write anything else.

My family—three children, their spouses, and eleven wonderful grandchildren, plus two grafted-in-by-marriage grandchildren—all of whom are the delights of my life and have encouraged and supported this MiMi beyond expectations.

Sharon—my exercise partner who read the manuscript, gave suggestions, and most of all prayed and rejoiced with me throughout the long, tedious journey of this project. Thanks for all your words of affirmation and the "atta girls" along the way.

Milton and Debbie—who have gone above and beyond the call of duty to invest in the ministry of this book. Your reward will be great in heaven—and, I believe, on this earth as well.

Kim—my talented and loving daughter who has honed her knowledge of punctuation and grammar from her years of homeschooling five intelligent boys. Thanks for pitching in to edit and making valuable story suggestions.

My faithful prayer partners and remarkable Victory Center family. I felt the encouragement of your prayers and support as this book developed and finally reached its completion.

The late Kenneth E. Hagin—our spiritual mentor—who helped pioneer the message of this book.

And finally, my Lord Jesus Christ who lived the story of this book and empowers us to make its message our own story.

Glossary of Hebrew Words Used

I have used many different names of God from the Hebrew, but each name refers to the one and only God. The various names bring out separate aspects of His character and indicate the variety of ways He interacts with mankind. Just as we in English refer to God as Almighty, Father, Lord, Master, Creator, etc., in the Hebrew text there are also many ways to refer to Jehovah. I have used these terms throughout this book to highlight the Jewish heritage of the characters and to add authenticity to the story.

Abba – Father

Addoni – Lord; Master

Chametz – leavening

El – God mighty strong and prominent

El Elyon – Most high

Elohim – God (plural); creator; preserver; transcendent; mighty; strong

Elohiym – Supreme God

El Shaddai – God Almighty; God All Sufficient

Haggadah – Jewish recitation during Passover

Jehovah – Jewish national name of God; The self-existent One; Lord God

Khamsin – a scorching hot, dry, dusty wind blowing from the desert during May through mid-June, and Sept. through Oct. lasting from 2 – 5 days.

Khawshak – loving delight

Kohanim – priests

Korban Pesach – Passover sacrifice; Passover lamb

Kosher – proper; legitimate; acceptable

Matzo – unleavened bread

Messiah – The Anointed One

Pesach – Passover

Rayah – companion; friend

Sanhedrin – council of seventy elders among the Jews who had the power of life and death

Sharav – another name for Khamsin

Yehweh – covenant name of God

Yeshua – Savior; Jesus in English

Prologue

Sydney, Australia, 1901

Death was everywhere—like an invisible predator stalking innocent prey; its greedy tentacles tearing into the bodies of victims, releasing venom throughout the bloodstream of young and old alike. Once the disease had a death grip, it would usually be only a matter of hours or days before the sufferer became a casualty of the bubonic plague.

As the nineteenth century flung open the door for the twentieth century to emerge, this specter of death crossed the threshold, shoving its way through unnoticed at first and then steadily gaining more notorious recognition.

Within just a few weeks, John had officiated more than forty funerals. And the sick and dying were everywhere in Sydney. He leaned his head against the window of the trolley car as he stared straight ahead with dazed eyes. Outside, the sullen Australia sky pelted the earth with a deluge of tears as though weeping at all its losses.

How can I endure if I have to bury another church member? he thought.

People were dying in such great numbers that the young minister was appalled. In many homes, little children, youths, and maidens were one by one stricken; then after struggling with intense agony in the throes of the dreadful disease, in the end, they lay cold and dead.

A tear slipped down John's cheek, reaching his beard before he could even summon the strength to fumble in his pocket for a handkerchief.

This outward display of emotion surprised him. He felt so numb from watching one after another of his precious church members suffer through the hideous symptoms of the plague that his senses seemed battered beyond feeling. Of the forty funerals he had performed, thirty of them had been from his own congregation. And now there would be another.

Long before sunup that morning, he had been awakened by a loud banging at the front door. When he had opened the door, he stared into the ashen face of his head deacon, Thomas Alcorn. Thomas looked as if it had been awhile since he'd slept. His face appeared drawn and haggard with bloodshot eyes enlarged with fear. He had nary a coat on, dressed only in a rumpled shirt and trousers held up by frayed suspenders.

"What are ya doin', mate?" John swiped his hand against his eyelids, struggling to maintain an awakened position.

"Ya got to come quick, Pastor." The urgency in Thomas's voice was unmistakable. "Sarah's mighty sickly."

He had clutched at John's arm. "I think it's the plague. Ya gotta come 'n pray for her." Thomas's voice broke as if stumbling over an invisible barrier.

With a sinking heart, John had thrown on some clothes and in the dark dashed the five blocks to where Thomas's sick wife lay. When they had entered the house, a stench assaulted his nostrils that threatened to empty his stomach. But the sight that greeted him as he rushed into the bedroom was beyond nauseating; it was revolting.

Sweat glistened on Sarah's feverish brow while her emaciated body shivered under piles of blankets. Her fingers clawed at deep, bluish buboes swelled to the size of hens' eggs in her armpits and on the sides of her neck. With eyes glazed over from lack of sleep, words spilled from her bloody lips that made no sense at all. John could tell that she was in intense pain by the way she thrashed back and forth on the bed.

The delirium had continued throughout the morning, and then shortly after the bell tolled at midday, her suffering had finally come to an end. Sure, John and Thomas had prayed. In fact, they had prayed and prayed. All morning they had wept and prayed. As the hours crept by, others had joined them, and they too had prayed. If fervency could have called down the healing hand of God, Sarah would have jumped up from that bed completely whole. But as it was, it appeared that either God had been deaf, or their prayers had reached no higher than the lamp hanging from the ceiling.

When it was all over, it seemed to John as if he could almost hear the triumphant mockery of evil fiends ringing in his ears as he had tried to speak words of Christian hope and consolation to the bereaved ones. One by one, the comforters had tried to make sense out of it all. Finally, some had offered the customary excuses as to why God had not come through for Sarah. Resorting to the traditional response, one recited with eyes lowered and much clicking of the tongue, "It must have been her time to go."

While another picked up the refrain, adding, "Yes, God just wanted to take her. It was his will that she cross over Jordan to her final dwelling place."

Others chimed in. "God needed her in heaven so he reached down and plucked her from this earth to be with him on the other side."

Never mind that her five children and husband, and even I, her pastor, needed her on this side.

Then, they had all departed, mumbling statements about how God works in mysterious ways, relieved that once again they had saved God's tarnished reputation and made the necessary justification for his lack of intervention.

Unfamiliar feelings of anger and frustration welled up inside of John as events from the last few hours paraded through his memory. He wasn't sure who he was angry with; he hoped it wasn't God. But somehow he suspected deep down he was in some way holding God responsible for the unfavorable outcome.

John was jarred into the present as the trolley car pulled to a stop a few blocks from the parsonage. He tried not to stomp down the aisle nor speak in a brusque tone when the driver wished him a good day, but he knew he probably had been unsuccessful considering his frame of mind.

The short way he had to walk in the pouring rain did nothing to lighten his mood. Jeanne couldn't help but hear the door slam as John burst through the front door.

She fairly ran down the hallway. "How is she?" she asked with deep concern etched across her face.

Jeanne looked as if she had been crying too. But as she reached up to help John remove his drenched hat and coat, she hesitated at the look that flashed across his face.

"She's dead, isn't she?"

John could only nod. His voice could not navigate past the huge lump stuck in his throat. He was in no mood to try to console his grief-stricken wife. However, throwing his dripping coat at the hook where it could dry, he gathered Jeanne in his arms to assure her that he really did care about what she was feeling. Then as soon as he could pull himself away from her clinging embrace, he headed for his study.

His disposition was suffering, and he had to get some answers. He and God were going to have it out, if it took all day, all night, or however long it took. God had some explaining to do.

John sat at his desk with his head bowed in sorrow; bitter tears flowed for all the afflicted people that had fallen under the ravages of that horrible disease. He wept until he finally felt some relief from the burning in his heart.

Then he prayed for some kind of message. Oh, how he longed to hear some explanation from him who had wept and sorrowed for suffering humanity long ago—from the one who had been a man of sorrows and acquainted with grief. How could it be God's will for his people to suffer so?

With hands lifted in supplication, he cried, "Why is this disease defiling and destroying the earthly temples of your children, O God?"

With a guttural cry of anguish from the depths of his heart, he shouted heavenward, "Is there no deliverer?"

Spent from his emotional tirade, John picked up his Bible. It had always comforted him before. Now he clung to it like a swimmer holding on to a lifeline to keep from being swept toward treacherous rocks by a vicious current.

The answer has to be in this book, John thought as he began his search through the familiar pages written a long time ago. He started to read. *In the beginning…*

Part One

Chapter One

In the Beginning

How could anything ever go wrong here? Eve looked around at her surroundings. What she saw was unspoiled in every way—spawned from the perfection of heaven itself. As far as the eye could see in every direction, the garden was picturesque and without flaw; it was, in fact, paradise. Still, she couldn't shake the unfamiliar feeling of unrest that had settled over her when she had awakened that morning. Something just didn't feel right, like a scratchiness that wouldn't go away.

Even as she watched the morning light paint the canvas of the dawn with artistic beauty, a blanket of foreboding dimmed her perception. Eve stood motionless, witnessing the introduction of a new day in the Garden of Eden. She breathed deeply, drinking in the serenity that the pageantry of colors offered fashioned by the hands of the Master Designer himself—nevertheless, she was still disturbed inside.

I wonder why I feel so different today. She absentmindedly trailed her fingers through Khawshak's velvety wool. The white sheep standing by her side nudged her elbow, demanding Eve's full attention. Reluctantly, she jerked her concentration from the mysterious sensation. Seeing Khawshak's upturned face alive with anticipation, she leaned over and tenderly rubbed the top of his head and then, impulsively, planted a kiss between his ears.

"Khawshak, you are a joy to have around." Eve tickled him playfully under his wooly chin. "What would I do without you? You really are a loving delight. That's what your name means, you know."

Eve lifted his large head so she could address him eye to eye. "If anything is amiss, it certainly isn't because of you." Lovingly, she stroked the stately white sheep that gazed up at her with adoring eyes.

Although Khawshak had been only a fuzzy ball of silken fleece when he was presented to Eve, now he had grown into a strong, muscular animal that stood well above her waist. He could easily have run her over when they enjoyed moments of playtime, but even though he was one of the lower forms of creation, Khawshak seemed to know he must be careful and respectful of this gentle mankind creature whom he loved devotedly.

"When Jehovah created you especially for me, he knew I would love you more than any of the other animals in the garden." Eve affectionately scratched Khawshak behind one ear as she shoved aside the strange feeling that threatened to influence her day. Instead, she gave a sigh of pleasure. Just thinking about her beloved Creator always caused praise to flow out of her effortlessly.

"Come on, Khawshak," Eve called in an effort to regain her normal lightheartedness as she headed down the path that led to a placid pool of water. A carpet of lush, viridian-green grass led up to the water's edge. Sprinkled here and there in the surrounding grassy meadow were clusters of flowers in every color and hue filling the atmosphere with their delicate fragrance.

As Eve and Khawshak approached the serene pool of water, the large sheep eagerly trotted to the water's edge and drank deeply. Eve seated herself beside Khawshak and gazed into the pond's mirrorlike surface. It always amazed her every time she caught a glimpse of her reflection; how could the Creator have formed what she saw from a bone out of Adam's side? With her finger she traced delicate features amid a smooth, creamy complexion. Long, thick lashes framed luminous, dark eyes that sparkled with vibrant life. As she bent over for a closer look, a shimmering cascade of long, black hair highlighted with auburn flecks fell around her face. She could barely detect the glow of divine radiant energy that constantly clothed her entire form.

A gentle breeze stirred the branches of an olive tree overhead, creating a symphony of subtle melodies. Ignoring the vague uneasiness that continued to linger, Eve stretched out in the cool grass. As she lay there, her thoughts jumped ahead to her favorite time of the day. She could sense excitement beginning to build as she anticipated the arrival of her Creator who always appeared in the cool of the evening without fail. What she and Adam eagerly looked forward to each time he came was the opportunity to bask in the pleasure of Jehovah's presence and enjoy a welcome interval of fellowship along with some much-needed orientation.

I know what I'll do, Eve thought. *I will ask Jehovah what this unusual sensation is. He knows everything.*

Relieved that she would soon find out what was going on, Eve closed her eyes to meditate on the goodness of the God whom she loved with a perfect love. At just the thought of his faithfulness, a flood of comforting warmth spread through every part of her being, overshadowing the heaviness that kept demanding her attention. In that state of quiet solitude, she must have dozed off because the next thing she knew, Khawshak was pressing his moist muzzle against her cheek.

"So, you are ready to go now, are you, little one?" Even though Khawshak was practically full grown, she had gotten in the habit of calling him "little one."

Eve arose to her feet and stretched gracefully. She never got tired of exploring the wonders of this magnificent garden where she and Adam lived. The garden stretched its boundless expanse in all directions with no end in sight. Already Eve knew it would take an immeasurable amount of time to explore it all.

She had seen parts of Eden with its ornate nooks artistically arranged with ornamental trees. Each area was decorated with living bouquets of brilliant flowers nestled against rocky ledges; some were complete with cascading waterfalls. And in other places she had discovered fountains of water shooting out sprays of tricolored mist surrounded by tall groves of fruit-laden trees of all colors and sizes. She had never detected any sign of corruption anywhere. Heavenly perfume saturated the environment, bathing each air molecule with a sweet-smelling blend of floral and spicy scents.

The Father had told them that there were four magnificent rivers that flowed from Eden, but Eve had only glimpsed one of them. Once, she and Adam had walked farther than usual and had seen massive mountains in the distance towering so high it looked as though their tops reached into the third heaven. There, they had caught sight of the northern bank of the mighty Pishon River. They had been told it coursed around the land of Havilah where gold, bdellium, and onyx stones were in abundance.

How long they had lived in this glorious place, she had no way of knowing—no way to measure time. Maybe they had been living in this ethereal paradise for an eternity, or maybe for just a day. But one thing she knew for sure: everything here was perfect, at least, that was what she had thought until now.

She couldn't describe how she had gotten here. Jehovah explained that she had been formed from a part of Adam's side, but she was not aware of any history or had any sense of yesterday. The present was what she knew best.

There were no limitations to the possibilities that lay before her and Adam. She was especially thankful that God in his infinite wisdom was always available to instruct and gently guide them into adventures beyond the scope of human imagination.

Shortly after they had been created, the first thing Eve remembered was standing before the great Jehovah completely immersed in the realization of his affection and acceptance. And then, he had spoken. She could never forget how the sound of that voice made her feel. It was powerful but gentle, authoritative and warm at the same time, leaving her feeling secure and loved.

Then Jehovah had blessed them. "Be fruitful, multiply, and fill the earth and subdue it with all its vast resources." He had said, "Adam and Eve, you have dominion over the fish of the sea, the birds of the air, and over every living creature that moves upon the earth."

The purposeful way Jehovah had delivered that command let Eve know those words might be the most important ones ever spoken in the universe.

She and Adam were to take dominion over all of creation—to expand its horizons and restore what evil had corrupted on the earth in eons past. Eve was aware that it was no small task they were assigned to, but she never questioned whether it was doable or not. No, with all the divine resources they had at their fingertips, of course, they would be successful. And as far as she knew, they had all the time in the world to make it happen.

For the greater part of the day, Eve and Khawshak meandered along the various trails, stopping now and then so Eve could sample fruit from different varieties of trees along the way when she felt hungry.

The sun had made its way to the heights of the heavens and was descending in its downward decline when they found that they had come to the center of the garden. Not far away, Eve caught a glimpse of her masculine counterpart—her husband, as Jehovah had called him. The feelings of warmth and belonging that Adam's presence stirred in her was a constant sense of wonder.

Her admiring gaze took in his wide, muscular shoulders and bronze, handsomely chiseled features. She loved to run her fingers through his hair that was as black as the raven that sat on the branch above her head. But it was not straight or coarse like the bird's feathers but wavy and shiny, reflecting the aura of the brilliant light that radiated from his powerfully built form.

As Eve watched Adam from a distance interacting with a huge gray animal decked out with large, floppy ears and a long, comical nose, her attention was drawn to the massive fruit-laden tree positioned in the exact center of the garden. Although stately in structure, the tree was surrounded with short, wiry bushes as though they were standing guard over it. And they might be at that because Jehovah had warned Adam against eating from that tree. It never crossed Eve's mind to give the tree any special attention. The Father had said it was off limits, and that was the end of the matter as far as she was concerned.

Slowly walking away from the center of the garden, Eve and Khawshak made their way along the familiar path that led to her favorite rose arbor. She had only gone a few paces when she heard an unfamiliar voice coming from a trail that made a sharp right turn off the main route. Curious as to who might have entered the garden undetected, she left Khawshak to graze while she veered from her intended course to investigate. Eve was so intent on following her curiosity that she failed to notice that the feeling of uneasiness inside had intensified.

There, poised in the middle of the thoroughfare, was a beautiful creature with iridescent skin of many colors covering his body. His eyes flashed as though on fire.

Without any introduction, the serpentlike creature spoke in a soft, seductive tone. "Can you eat of the fruit from all these trees?"

Eve was amazed to hear the strange animal speak. None of the other animals in the garden had the ability to carry on a conversation; right away, Eve could tell this one was uniquely different. Thinking maybe the creature was hungry and needed some food, Eve offered willingly, "Oh, yes! The Father has abundantly supplied all of these wonderful trees to furnish us with many varieties of fruit." Then she hesitated. "That is, except that huge tree in the middle of the garden. We are not allowed to even so much as touch it, or we shall die."

Even as Eve was freely giving out the information that her husband had passed on to her, in her mind she was thinking for the first time, *I wonder what it means to die?*

She had always just taken for granted that if the tree was forbidden, then who was she to question Jehovah?

She was so surprised at the question that had come into her mind and so completely engrossed in her thoughts that she failed to notice the unearthly gleam that appeared in the serpent's eyes as he focused on the tree Eve had pointed out.

Very carefully, the creature began to work his way closer to the notable tree as he spoke with all the conviction and persuasiveness of the wisest of sages. "No, child, you won't die." Then in a hushed, secretive tone, he questioned, "Do you know why God doesn't want you to eat the fruit of that tree?"

"I'm…I'm not sure." Eve hesitated. She had never wondered before. Up to this point, she knew nothing about the tree except that it was called the Tree of the Knowledge of Good and Evil. She knew well enough what good was, but evil—well, she had no idea what that was. The term meant nothing to her. Now she was intrigued. This conversation was proving to be very interesting.

The dazzling creature shifted his position so that Eve could have full view of the extraordinary tree. "God knows if you eat the fruit from that tree." He paused and then extended his upper appendage in a graceful, fluid motion, pointing in the direction of the tree. With the flourish of an orator, he lowered his hypnotic voice for emphasis and added, "You will become just like *God*!"

When the creature said *God*, the repulsion with which he said it created such an explosion of force from his mouth that Eve stumbled backward a step and had to steady herself by grabbing hold of the trunk of the nearby sycamore tree. The booming voice continued. "The fruit hanging there will give you all the knowledge that God has." He lowered his voice to almost a whisper, and in a deliberate and measured manner, like a persuader presenting his final argument, he said, "Then, of course, you wouldn't need to wait until he shows up. You could do it all by yourself."

While the creature was speaking, Eve had been aware that early on in the conversation, Adam had positioned himself close behind her, but she was so fascinated by the presence of this curious animal that she didn't even turn to acknowledge him. Evidently, Adam was just as intrigued because he said nothing.

Actually, Eve had never heard firsthand the sober commandment concerning this extraordinary tree. All she had to go on was Adam's word, for God had given the instructions to him before she had come on the scene. She just assumed Adam knew what he was talking about and had trusted him completely.

But now, well, since he wasn't saying anything, maybe he wasn't exactly sure of the rules and God's motive behind this strange restriction after all. Maybe they really didn't know Jehovah their Father as well as they thought they did. He was gone all day, and then without fail, he always showed up in the evening. What did he do during the daytime, and why was he so mysterious?

Of course, when the Father was there in the garden, it was always the most enjoyable time of the day, and never mind that his presence permeated the garden all the time. What if Jehovah had a hidden agenda—withholding some vital information that they needed? Heaven knew that their knowledge was limited. When they wanted to know something of importance, they always had to ask the Father. Come to think of it, that had been kind of inconvenient.

Ignoring the inner warning that was trying to get her attention, Eve edged closer to the barrier of bushes that encircled the fascinating tree and for the first time actually examined it. She allowed her eyes to absorb the lush display of verdant foliage loaded with delectable fruit, which dangled from low-hanging branches. Each piece of fruit still glistened with the morning dew, enhancing the luminous hues of crimson, orange, and gold, making it delightful to behold.

As Eve leaned even closer in the direction of the forbidden tree, she caught a whiff of the tantalizing aroma emanating from the intriguing harvest just within reach. As her senses became captivated with this exhilarating discovery, something stirred inside that she had never felt previously. It was an intense longing not awakened before mixed with a dart of passion that inflamed something within. Instinctively, Eve knew if she allowed that feeling to take over, she could experience pleasure unlike any she had known in all her existence. Even the fact that the fruit was forbidden created a fascinating excitement that was titillating.

She sensed that Adam, who had drawn closer to the tree, was also feeling what she was experiencing. Eve suspected they were on the verge of moving into a realm of enhanced consciousness that for some unknown reason Jehovah had tried to keep as a secret from them. Funny how none of this had happened before that beguiling serpentlike creature had shown up. In fact, his very nearness exuded a certain enlightenment that was deliciously exhilarating, totally different from the awesome sensations produced by the presence of Jehovah.

As though perceiving exactly what Eve was thinking, the incandescent being glided into position between Eve and the sentinel bushes. Cleverly manipulating the twisted branches, he opened up a convenient pathway that allowed unhindered access to the tempting fruit. Directing Eve's focus toward the inviting array, he dramatically pointed toward the tree. "Look what you have been missing out on. These delicious delicacies have been here all along, just ripe for the taking."

Bowing low, he gave Eve a slight nudge through the passageway. "See what Jehovah has been withholding from you."

Then, confiding in a mysterious tone, he said, "Jehovah just doesn't want you to enjoy yourself and certainly doesn't want you to become like him or have the knowledge he has. Actually, I happen to know, firsthand, that Jehovah doesn't like competition. He thinks he is God and doesn't want anyone else to challenge him. If you eat from that tree, you will have as much knowledge as he has." Then he announced with emphasis, "You both will be gods just like him."

Eve hesitated for only a moment then took a tentative step in the direction of the forbidden tree. Glancing sideways at Adam who stood at her right, she could tell he was spellbound by the serpent and was not going to make any move to stop her. Slowly, she entered the passageway through the bushes, and then, as though some invisible force was luring her forward, she felt a magnetism that caused her to hasten toward the prize that now hung just beyond her fingertips.

Quickly, she plucked the tempting piece of fruit closest to her before she would allow herself to think about it anymore. Nothing changed. There was no indication that this *death* Jehovah had warned them of had happened. In fact, she felt even more empowered than ever. So without waiting any longer, she bit into the tender morsel, savoring the delicious honey-like taste of succulent fruit that fairly melted on her tongue. The flavor was indeed pleasurable. Before she took another bite, however, she noticed Adam had followed her to the tree. Turning to him, she offered a sample, and without hesitation, he too ate of the fruit.

No sooner had Adam consumed a bite of the forbidden fruit than they both heard an eerie reverberation behind them. When they whirled around to see where the sound came from, what they saw made them tremble. In the spot where the seductive creature had previously stood was a manifestation unlike any they had seen before. The serpent that had just moments before been so convincing in all of its magnificent beauty now was positioned in front of them, looking both grotesque and repulsive. The creature that had appeared to be so enticing was now hideous and revolting.

They rubbed their eyes; they couldn't believe what they were seeing. A second look confirmed that indeed the creature had changed, or had he been like that all the time, and they had just been blinded to the truth? Eve was confused. What was happening?

"In the day you eat of it, your eyes will be opened. You will know the difference between good and evil." That's what they had been told earlier, and now that pronouncement echoed in

Eve's ears. Suddenly, knowing the difference between good and evil didn't seem so appealing.

Tearing her eyes away from the frightening creature, she thought, *So that is what evil looks like.*

She shuddered as she vehemently cast what was left of the iniquitous fruit as far as she could throw it. But changes had not only happened to the serpent; Eve could tell immediately that something had been altered inside of her as well. Even though the sun was just as bright as before, inside, Eve felt as though darkness had permeated her whole being, causing a strange oppression and heaviness.

Turning to Adam, she sobbed, "Oh, Adam, what have we done?"

As tears spilled down her cheeks, she lifted her eyes to look into the face of her beloved husband. She drew back in horror at the transformation that had taken place in Adam. Before, a glorious aura of light had covered them both; but now, the radiance was gone. Adam stood before her stark naked. Even the kind twinkle of joy and adoration that had always lit up his eyes—especially when he looked at her—was replaced with a vacant look of hopelessness and confusion; but worst of all, he was staring at her with an accusing glare.

Eve could tell by the look on Adam's face that the changes she had seen in him had also taken place in her. She was naked, and beyond that, she was dreadfully ashamed. For the first time in her life, she didn't know what to do. The unfamiliar sensation of fear gripped her. When anything unusual had come about in the past, instinctively, she would know exactly what to do each time. And if there were any questions at all, she had the comforting assurance that she could always ask the Father when he came each evening for fellowship.

The Father. Oh, no! It would not be long before his regular visit. The last thing I want to do now is face him naked like this. Eve looked down at her unclothed body and shivered.

"Do you think Jehovah will know what we have done?" Eve hung her head in embarrassment as she addressed Adam, avoiding his eyes.

"Well, what do you think, woman? Of course he will know. He knows everything."

Eve recoiled at the harshness in Adam's tone of voice. At his abrupt reply, a stab of pain hit the pit of her stomach that threatened to cause her to double over at its intensity. On top of the anguish she was feeling from guilt, this new pain was almost more than she could bear.

Sobbing hysterically, Eve whirled around and ran. Without even a glance, she darted past the despicable creature that had caused the entire cataclysm. He had stationed himself close by, relishing with fiendish elation the triumph of his evil plan. Eve rushed blindly on until she collapsed in a grove of fig trees. There she curled up in a ball and wept in despair.

She didn't know how long she had lain in that pitiful condition before she heard a rustling in the bushes behind where she lay. Wearily, Eve lifted her head only to see Adam edging his way into the clearing. His tall form towered over her, causing a different kind of fear to surface.

"We've got to do something," Adam murmured dully. Hardly looking at Eve, he grabbed her arm and jerked her to a standing position.

Eve could see fear in Adam's countenance too, even though he was trying desperately to hide it behind a gruff, stern demeanor.

"You know Jehovah will be here soon. We can't let him see us in this condition." Adam looked around with determined resolve. Reaching up, he grabbed a fistful of fig leaves from the branch that hovered over his head.

"Maybe we can do something with these." Clumsily, he twisted the fig leaves this way and that, but try as he might, he couldn't get them to stay together long enough to do any good.

Hardly raising her voice above a whisper, Eve offered, "Here, let me try." As she carefully took the leaves from Adam's hands, she surveyed the surrounding area. Finding some gently trailing vines that had worked their way up over a boulder, she stripped them of their leaves and by tying each leaf together with the flexible cords was able to make some crude coverings.

Adam and Eve had just donned the makeshift garments that Eve had fashioned when they heard a familiar sound. Normally, the sound of the rushing wind that signaled the arrival of Jehovah was welcomed with delightful anticipation. But today, that was the last thing Adam and Eve wanted to hear. Where previously great waves of pure love had engulfed them at the mere thought of Jehovah's presence, now all they felt was stark terror. With the fear came tormenting thoughts of impending punishment and doom.

Crouching among the trees, Adam and Eve hid themselves from the presence of the Lord God Jehovah. They waited for what seemed an eternity until finally they heard the booming, authoritative voice of God call out, "Adam! Where are you?"

Eve whispered, "Don't say anything. Maybe he won't be able to find us and go away."

"Don't be stupid," Adam snapped. "He knows where we are. He just wants us to reveal our whereabouts. We've got to face him sooner or later, anyway. We might as well get it over with."

With that, Adam stepped out from the shelter of the fig trees and resolutely marched into the vicinity of his Creator. Eve crept up behind him trying to look brave, but her fearful demeanor betrayed her.

Not waiting for Jehovah to have an opportunity to say anything, Adam hurriedly began to explain their tardiness.

"You see…I…that is, we…" Adam faltered, then in a determined effort to finish quickly added, "I heard the sound of you walking in the garden, and I was afraid because I was naked, so I hid myself." There, he had said it.

Adam and Eve didn't see the look of disappointment and sorrow on Jehovah's countenance because now for the first time, they were unable to stand to look at him. However, when he began to speak, they could hear the grief in his voice as he asked, "Who told you that you were naked? Have you eaten of the tree of which I commanded that you should not eat?"

They really didn't know the answer to the first question, but the answer to the second one, they knew only too well.

Adam was quick to speak up again. "The woman you gave to me"—he turned and pointed an accusing finger at the now cowering Eve—"she gave me fruit of the tree, and I ate of it."

Turning to Eve, Jehovah tenderly addressed her. "What is this you have done?"

Eve hung her head in shame as she stammered. "The-the… ah…serpent…." Looking around, she spotted the loathsome beast gleefully observing the melodrama that was unfolding. Pointing in his direction, Eve continued, "He beguiled and deceived me, and I ate the fruit."

Jehovah gave the serpentlike creature a long, knowing look. Suddenly, his eyes blazed like a flame of fire, and out of his mouth, power erupted as though his words were a sharp sword. Then with the fierceness of his wrath and the indignation of a righteous, almighty God, he addressed the serpent with such force that the earth beneath their feet began to quake. "Because you have done this, you are cursed above all animals and above every living thing of the field; upon your belly you shall go, and you shall eat dust all the days of your life."

And then, as though Jehovah had changed his focus from the snakelike animal to an invisible being that was hiding inside, he proclaimed, "I will put enmity between you and the woman and between your offspring and her offspring; he shall bruise your head under foot, and you will lie in wait and bruise his heel."

The explosion of authority that accompanied the words that proceeded from the mouth of God produced such a mighty force that the serpent was propelled backward. Twisting and turning, he finally flipped over on his belly and quickly slithered away into the bushes. All of his appendages had disappeared, and he was completely covered with ugly scales from head to tail. He was no longer able to communicate but instead was filled with deadly venom left behind by the former occupant of his body.

The invisible spirit that had inhabited the serpent's body, however, departed with a malicious, raucous laugh of triumph that resounded throughout the first and second heavens. Despite the sober pronouncement from God hinting at his defeat, his plan had worked—at least for now.

Eve wasn't aware of all of the ramifications of what they had just witnessed, but with her newly acquired knowledge of evil, she knew that something cruel and vicious had been released on the earth that could not be reversed.

Unbearable regret gripped her with such intensity that she fell to the ground prostrate. Her mind gradually began to comprehend knowledge of the punishment of death that Jehovah had warned them about. Now she knew. The guilt that had stolen her sense of fellowship with the perfect love of the Father, the self-consciousness that caused her to focus on her own nakedness, the shame of failure, the self-incrimination, the pain of rejection, and the all-consuming fear that had taken up resident within her was *death*.

The glorious connection to Jehovah had been severed—the very source of life—now there was nothing else to look forward to except the continuation of death's influence and the end thereof. She did not know what that outcome would be. Hopelessness, decay, and darkness loomed ahead with no remedy.

☼ Chapter Two

Time and nature seemed to stand still as the Creator of the universe turned to Adam and Eve—the crown of his creation—to pass the inevitable judgment that they knew was coming. His majestic form was no longer able to be detected by their human eyes. All that was visible was a light that was so brilliant that the only thing they could do was lay prostrate on the ground trembling in fear. But they could hear the voice—the voice that used to comfort and bless them was now preparing to pronounce sentence, not from the position of a loving Father anymore, but instead from the standpoint of a righteous judge.

Eve could feel the rushing wind that had accompanied the arrival of Jehovah change into a howling tempest filled with the fury of eternal condemnation. Even the birds that had filled the Garden with their endless melodies were silent as though holding their songs in sorrow at what was to come.

Finally, after what seemed like eons of torment, God began to speak once again. In a voice filled with grief yet exhibiting stern resolve, he said, "Eve, I will greatly multiply your suffering in pregnancy and with spasms of distress you will bring forth children. Yet your desire and craving will be for your husband, and he will rule over you."

Eve already had some knowledge of what childbearing was. She had watched various animals produce tiny replicas of themselves and had seen them begin to grow and mature. Because Jehovah had instructed her and Adam to be fruitful and multiply, she had eagerly looked forward to the time when she too could hold her first little human child in her arms—in fact, the yearning had been growing stronger for some time.

At least I am still going to be able to have children, Eve thought with a small measure of relief. But for the first time, she was becoming acquainted with pain; mixing anguish with the greatest joy she could imagine during childbirth did seem like a hard affliction to endure.

As for the rest of the indictment about her husband, she wasn't sure what that would entail. In the past, it had been effortless to want to please her husband, but now, since all this had happened, he almost seemed like a hard taskmaster without compassion. Eve suspected that nothing was going to be easy from that point on.

Then Jehovah spoke again, and this time his voice took on a more authoritative tone as he addressed Adam. "Because you have given heed to the voice of your wife and have eaten of the tree of which I commanded you, saying, you shall not eat of it, the ground is under a curse because of you; in sorrow and toil shall you eat of the fruits of it all the days of your life. Thorns also and thistles shall it bring forth for you, and you shall eat the plants of the field. In the sweat of your face shall you eat bread until you return to the ground, for out of it you were taken; for dust you are, and to dust you shall return."

When God had finished his bleak edict to Adam, Eve felt him stiffen beside her and let out a wretched moan. She suspected he was feeling the oppressive weight of having to provide for the needs of his decendants without the benefit of the glorious anointing that had made all of his tasks so trouble free up until then.

Adam and Eve lay under the influence of the weight of Jehovah's holy justice for a space of time unable to find the strength to move. Then once again, the voice of God commanded, "Arise! Stand upright on your feet."

Painstakingly, with all the effort they could muster, Adam and Eve struggled to stand. When finally they were able to remain upright, their pitiful excuse for covering slipped to the ground and lay in shambles at their feet, like a mass of refuse useless in its frailty to hide the uncleanness of guilt.

Naked once again, they cowered before their God not able to imagine what was coming next, but with a certain knowing that it would include misery and even tragedy.

Suddenly, Adam and Eve sensed the tangible presence of Jehovah recede from the atmosphere, and timidly, they lifted their eyes to where he had been. In his place stood a man not unlike them in shape and form but with a countenance radiant and awesome. He was clothed with a robe that reached to his feet and a girdle of gold about his breast. His hair was white like wool, and his eyes flashed like a flame of fire. His feet glowed like bright, burnished bronze as if it had been refined in a furnace, and his voice was like the sound of many waters. As he spoke, his words were like a sharp two-edged sword, and his face shone as bright as the sun at midday.

"I have loved you with an everlasting love," he said with hands extended toward Adam and Eve as though wanting to embrace them. "With loving-kindness have I drawn you and have continued my faithfulness to you so that you lacked for nothing, yet you did not obey your Father's command."

He then let his arms drop to his side as a pained expression filled his eyes. "Your sin is great, and now you are cut off from the everlasting life that has sustained you." Slowly, a tear slipped from eyes full of compassion and trickled down his cheek until it fell to the earth from which Adam and Eve had been formed.

He then continued with great feeling mixed with grim resolve. "Every sin has dire consequences; therefore, the soul that sins must die." He finished with the sober finality of a judge relegating a criminal to a sentence of certain doom.

There was that word die *again,* Eve thought. *God said if we would eat fruit from the tree of the knowledge of good and evil that we would surely die. But so far, all that has happened has been a dramatic change in our appearance and dire predictions for the future. But death?*

Eve was still not sure what that meant. However, at that thought, an overpowering dread took possession of her as she anxiously waited for what terrible event would happen next.

Everything seemed surreal to Eve until she felt the cold nose of Khawshak rub against her bare leg. Forcing her attention from the commanding figure that stood before them, she let her arm fall across the sheep's broad neck, drawing comfort for the first time from his nearness.

At the God-man's final pronouncement, a silence filled the garden with a stillness that could be felt, like the calm before a devastating storm. Not a leaf moved; not an animal made a sound; and even the grass ceased swaying, as though nature was holding its breath, waiting.

Once again, Eve turned her gaze toward the magnificent man. She was surprised to see that his focus had changed from her and Adam, and now his attention was fixed on Khawshak. Khawshak was looking back at the man as though there were some unspoken communication going on between the two.

Abruptly, Eve felt the lamb jerk his head out from under her arm and methodically make his way forward until he was standing directly in front of the being. Then without any prompting, Khawshak meekly dropped to the ground and lay submissively at his feet.

Eve rushed to Khawshak's side and flung her arms around his neck. "Khawshak! What are you doing?" Once again, a horrible pang of fear shot through her belly. Somehow, she had an instinctive premonition of what was taking place. "Get up," she pleaded with a terrified cry as she looked frantically at the man who towered over them. Khawshak only gazed at Eve with eyes full of resolve and then turned his head as a final gesture of determination.

Gently, the God-man lifted Eve to her feet and tenderly led her to where her husband still stood. Adam encircled her with his arms and drew Eve to his side as she sobbed uncontrollably.

Hiding her face in his chest, they both turned from the foreboding scene and just clung to each other.

Then the magnificent being announced with an empathy that resonated beyond that present age. "No one has greater love than to lay down his own life for his friends."

With that, there was a swish like the descent of a swift, sharp sword. Khawshak made no sound as he willingly paid the ultimate sacrifice for the sin of his beloved.

As his blood flowed, those watching from the eternal, heavenly realm gazed down through the corridors of time to another lamb who, centuries later, would voluntarily lay down his life. Then, it would not be a covering for just two humans; instead, his blood would pay for the sins of the whole human race.

Meanwhile, Adam and Eve felt as though their grief had propelled them into a new and different region—one of intense sorrow, heaviness, and darkness, full of confusion and most of all fear. Even though they were still surrounded by beauty and light, there was no joy in their hearts anymore, just unbearable defeat and hopelessness.

What was going on behind them, Eve did not know, nor did she want to know. She suspected her beloved Khawshak was gone, and it was all because of her. Again, she wept until no more tears would come. Still, the emptiness refused to subside, and a new wave of guilt and regret threatened to overpower her.

Then from behind them, they once again heard the voice of the mysterious being. This time, there was a note of hope in his voice as he spoke. "Blessed is he who has forgiveness of his transgression—whose sin is covered."

Can sin be covered? Eve wondered through her misery. *What's done is done. How then could it ever be undone? This man who seemed so like God had said that someone who sins must die. What they had done had to be what he was referring to as sin.*

She sensed that the one who had just spoken had drawn near to the spot where they stood huddled together. They hesitantly turned around. When Eve finally found the courage to lift her head enough to behold the glorious being standing in front of them, she stared into eyes that looked like two bottomless pools of love. His countenance radiated kindness as he held out to them two garments that he had fashioned from the sacrificial lamb that they had loved so dearly.

As he clothed them with the bloodstained garments, Eve staggered at the revelation of the horrible consequences of sin. What an enormously high price had been paid so that their sin could be forgiven. Was there no other atonement adequate for their horrible sin than the life of an innocent being: Khawshak's life for theirs? Now Eve knew why Khawshak had so willingly laid down his life for them—he loved them. That was it, pure and simple.

As Eve allowed her eyes to shift to where the lifeless body of Khawshak lay, she grasped for the first time that love was the remedy for sin. Not a love that was shallow and trivial, but a love that was so complete and unending that it was willing to sacrifice its whole being for the one that was loved. Finally, Eve knew what the final outcome of death was, but at the same time, she was also beginning to understand the powerful meaning of undeserved forgiveness.

As Eve caught sight of Khawshak's body, now so pitiful and still, a seed of life began to spring up in her heart. For the first time since she had fallen for that horrible deception, she saw a spark of light. Hope burst through the emptiness of her soul. Somehow, the guilt that had gripped her was being replaced with a flood of thankfulness and love—not only for the one who had laid down his life for their sin, but also for her Creator who had made a way to escape the full consequences of their disobedience.

Now she knew. The evil that had been unleashed into the world through their disobedience did have a remedy. Yes, it would be messy and painful, but because love was the most powerful force in the universe, then love would someday prevail over evil.

Chapter Three

Centuries passed. And year after year, decade after decade, the wickedness of mankind became great in the earth. Every imagination and intention of all human thinking was only evil continually. The iniquity that Adam and Eve had released in the world had taken its toll. The human race was now familiar with evil in every aspect while the knowledge of good was slowly fading into the archives of history.

The Lord God Jehovah regretted that he had made man and was sorely grieved in his heart at what he was witnessing. The chaos in an almost loveless society was unrestrained by human kindness and mercy. It pained the loving heart of the heavenly Father to watch his prized creation suffer under the oppressive canopy of the curse that sin had brought into the world.

• •

But not so for Lucifer, the Devil, or Satan as he was now called; he, who had become the seducer and deceiver of all humanity, finally had achieved his goal. At last, he had weaseled authority away from God and had become ruler over a kingdom. By convincing Adam to sin—who had been given dominion over the earth—authority had been handed over to him. Now this mastermind of evil had become the undisputed ruler of the earth. Finally Satan had authority over something. Never mind that it wasn't over the entire universe like God, but at last he was the prince of the power of the air on planet earth.

In eons past when he had been known as the Morning Star and referred to as a Shining One, he had had great aspirations. It had not been enough for him to be one of the three highest ranking archangels in the heavenly realm; his ambition was to be like God.

No, actually, he desired to be above God and rule the whole universe. Why settle for second best? He had set his sights on supremacy. Lucifer had been beautiful enough and convincingly ingenious enough to collect quite a following among the heavenly beings that admired and respected his leadership. He had had a foolproof plan for a revolt that would propel him into becoming the supreme power of the universe—or so he thought.

Lucifer's strategy had been simple: enlist as many angels as he could; take over the strategic areas of heaven; dethrone God and cast him out into the timeless wastelands of the universe; and conquer and subdue all of his loyal followers.

Lucifer was just proud enough to think that his plan would succeed, but he had underestimated the infinite power of an omnipotent God. When he had faced off with the mighty Jehovah, only one blast of his breath and one power-filled word from God's mouth had produced a force that had struck Lucifer with such intensity that it felt like he had been sliced apart with a two-edged sword. Instantly, Michael and his angelic hosts had flown into action. The war that had broken out in heaven between Lucifer's seditious band and Michael's angelic armies was brutal but short-lived.

Lucifer—the huge dragon, the ages-old serpent, the one who was to become the seducer and deceiver of all humanity—was forced out of heaven, and his angels were flung out along with him. They fell in a thunderous roar burning with a great fire like lightning falling from heaven. They had been soundly defeated, and there was no room found for them in heaven any longer.

For Satan, the epoch of time that followed was a period of overwhelming humiliation as he had experienced degradation in the eyes of his disgraced troops. He seethed with anger and bitterness as he wandered aimlessly throughout the dry places of creation, stirring up a cauldron of mayhem that ripped apart and destroyed the planet earth to which they had been exiled. The influence of their hideous rebellion had produced a cacophony of evil and darkness that blanketed the planet, reducing it to a wasteland without form and totally void of life.

Nothing changed for eons until in the midst of the darkness and the murderous uproar in the atmosphere surrounding the dark planet, Satan heard a sound. It was a noise like a rushing mighty wind. He had heard that sound many times while in heaven; it was easily recognizable as the hovering presence of the Holy Spirit. A chill had gone down his twisted spine. Hordes of evil spirit beings huddled together in frightened clusters round about him. What was happening?

Then he heard a voice reverberate throughout the heavens. It was a voice he had been all too familiar with. A voice that made him shudder and tremble at the memories it stirred up. God was speaking.

"Let there be light."

And there was light.

Darkness was Satan and his angel's habitat of choice because their deeds were evil. They were wicked through and through and could not operate or traffic in light. In fact, light was painful and disorienting to their activities. But at God's command, light exploded everywhere. Hurriedly, they scrambled into the space above the earth's atmosphere where they were packed together like sardines in the only dark region that was available at that time.

Day after day, they watched in horror as God, the Word, and the Holy Spirit systematically recreated life and beauty on the formerly God-forsaken planet. Elohim had even gone so far as to form a special garden strategically located on the earth's surface, especially resplendent in its glory.

But their interest increased when on the sixth day, God, the Word, and the Holy Spirit seemed to be involved in a particularly mystifying activity. Out of the dust of the ground they were fashioning a creature that looked alarmingly like God himself. The whole procedure had their undivided attention. Later, when the Creator extracted a part of the creature he had made and subsequently formed another smaller one similar to the first, the hosts of darkness were bewildered. What was God up to, anyway?

Satan had been engrossed in watching the drama that was unfolding when unexpectedly he overheard a conversation between the Creation Team and those two strange beings.

"Be fruitful and multiply," God had commanded, "and fill the earth, and subdue it using all its vast resources and have dominion over the fish of the sea, the birds of the air, and over every living creature that moves upon the earth."

Those newly created beings might not have known the full significance of what God was telling them, but Satan knew. God was giving those two undeveloped creatures full authority over planet Earth. How stupid could God be to make those earthborn entities a little lower than God himself and then to crown them with such glory and honor?

For the first time since his expulsion from heaven, a fiendish grin spread across Satan's vile face. His time had finally come. His first plan had failed, but this time, he would find a way to seize that coveted authority and take over as prince and ruler of the earth. The thought had a delicious ring to it. Furthermore, he would give God a significant slap in the face by corrupting his creation and in the process once again firmly position himself as an esteemed leader in the eyes of the disgusting group of evil beings that had been foolish enough to follow him.

And as he had predicted, Satan's plan had been successful. With authority legally transferred into his hands and an army of villainous beings ready to carry out his undisputed orders, he sat up his throne in the second heaven and commenced to kill, steal, and destroy at will. The whole world was under the power of this evil one, and systematically, once again, the earth was being brought back to its former state of darkness and lawlessness—the only condition that Satan and his cohorts were comfortable with.

There was one thing that bothered Satan. After he had deceived Adam and Eve, the seemingly prophetic words that God had spoken to him on that occasion appeared troubling. The seed of woman was supposed to crush his head.

"No! That couldn't happen," he reasoned. Ever since Adam and Eve had sinned, each child that had been born thereafter had the seed of rebellion structured into his genetic lineage, positioning each one of them firmly under his authority. There certainly was no one who had any power over him.

As the centuries unfolded with very few serious setbacks to Satan's undisputed agenda, he managed to establish a highly developed, structured kingdom. One of his most promising projects had taken place in the plains of Shinar where his collection of human pawns had settled down. As a result of Satan's covert influence, they had all agreed to build a tower that would reach to the heavens intending to create a centralized monument of worship for their gods. Satan was ecstatic. Finally he was going to receive the adulation he deserved.

But just as he was preening for his opening début, something disturbing happened. His chief adversary had to mess up his well-organized scheme. Jehovah stuck his finger in the pot and stirred it up by confounding the languages of Satan's unified band of human hostages, preventing them from understanding one another's speech. Well, that ended that. They scattered here and there unable to accomplish what they had started.

Then a few centuries later, Satan encountered another troubling situation. God laid down a series of laws to a motley congregation of Hebrews. Satan discovered that if those people were able to obey the rules to the letter, their sins were covered because of the blood of all those lambs they had been commanded to sacrifice. It was terribly unsettling when he found that in those cases his authority had little effect. In fact, when those laws were kept correctly, the angelic hosts protected and fought for them, thwarting his plans at every turn. That was downright annoying to say the least. But his head was still intact, and no one had had the ability to crush it and would not succeed as long as he still had authority over planet earth.

Still, Satan was wary. God was not a being that could be trifled with. That damnable prophecy was hanging over his head. It would not pay to be caught off guard. He was the ruler of the present darkness that covered the world, and he would do what it took to stay that way no matter who or what tried to stop him. He wasn't about to quit.

However, Satan's alarm went off when the Jewish prophets started spouting off, hinting that someone was coming that would redeem mankind out of Satan's clutches. Evidently, God had something really big planned—something that Satan had to find out about before he wound up with his head crushed.

The first clue that God's plan was unfolding was when *that baby* was born; the one that was to be produced by a virgin who had never been impregnated by the seed of a man. Sure enough, it had happened just like the prophets had predicted. Satan could see that this child could produce a new set of difficulties for him. A child that was not contaminated with Adam's seed was in a different category than he had ever dealt with before—except for Adam and Eve of course.

Satan had tried to wipe the child out while he was just a baby through one of his murderous puppets, but Herod, the bumbling idiot that he was, had botched the opportunity. He had succeeded in killing a lot of innocent babies, however, so Satan had gotten a measure of satisfaction from the blood, mayhem, and horrendous amount of pain it had caused.

But for thirty years, as figured by earthly time, Satan had lost track of that special baby—until now. Just a few days ago, the voice of God had thundered from heaven. Of all places, it had happened east of Jericho at the southern part of the Jordan River where that lunatic preacher they called John the Baptist had been baptizing sinners. Satan's emissaries had set up surveillance at that spot because Satan had suspected this man might be the one he had been looking for. However, his efforts had been rewarded when he observed another quite different man approaching this wild-eyed preacher. Satan shuddered when he overheard the pronouncement declaring that innocent-looking man to be the Lamb of God that could take away the sins of the world. But then what happened next shook Satan to his core. A thunderous voice from heaven announced in no uncertain terms: "This is my beloved Son in whom I am well pleased!"

Aha! So that was the plan. Of course, the one whom Satan had known as the Word when he had been in heaven now was present on the earth in human form. Whatever the plan was, this man must be destroyed one way or the other.

Oh, well, Satan thought. *I have succeeded in deceiving and seducing the first man that God created; this one will be no different. And even though he is God in the flesh, he is in the flesh. And that will be his downfall.*

Chapter Four

Sydney, Australia

John rubbed his eyes, bloodshot from the tears he had shed and weary from reading. Pushing his chair back from his desk, he let his Bible fall shut. Outside, the rain had subsided to a gentle tapping on the window pane. Late afternoon shadows cloaked the rain-drenched streets and gutters with a shroud of gray. From the direction of the kitchen, the tantalizing aroma of meat smothered with onions and garlic extended to him a delicious invitation. John's stomach responded as if on cue.

How long had it been since he had eaten? He could just vaguely remember grabbing a morsel of bread as he had rushed out the door that morning. Sarah's death had so taken away his appetite that the very thought of food had made his stomach rebel. But now he was hungry.

Maybe a little break is what I need. John stood and ran his fingers through his already disheveled hair, gripping its strands in frustration. He still hadn't found the answers to the flood of questions that had bombarded his mind—and yes, even his faith. He had meant it when he had demanded answers from God, no matter how long it would take to get them. He had to know. Why was God doing this to them? John had been faithful—at least as devoted as he knew how to be. And Sarah had been loyal to the faith—the very epitome of a godly wife and mother. And yet God had taken her along with so much of his congregation. Why?

That very word wrapped its tentacles around John's heart threatening to squeeze the life out of it. The darkness descending in the world outside his study window seemed to parallel the gloom moving stealthily upon his soul.

Why bother to do what is right and run myself ragged doing the work of the Lord if this is how I get rewarded? John banged his fist on the desk. He despised the feeling of bitterness and had always worked hard to keep it at bay in the past. But now—he could sense it shoving its way into his mind coming dangerously close to penetrating his heart.

John shook his head forcefully as if movements alone could dislodge those uncomfortable thoughts. But they wouldn't budge. Okay. He was angry at God. There, he had finally admitted it. Not mad enough to shake his fist at the Almighty—at least not yet, but John was plenty upset with his Creator nevertheless.

What have we done to deserve this? John gritted his teeth and then let out a groan that erupted from the anguish boiling in his heart. He was just considering burying his face in his hands once more and giving way to the sobs that were building up inside when he heard a timid knock on the door.

"John, are you all right?" John could tell that Jeanne was concerned by the tone of her voice.

"Sure. I'm fine." John tried to pull himself together while he crossed the room to open the door.

"Your supper is ready." John could tell by the look on Jeanne's face that she really didn't believe he was anywhere close to being all right.

"Give me just a minute, and I'll be there." Human company was not what he wanted right then, but neither did he want to trouble Jeanne any more than she already was. He would struggle through a meal and then get back to the task at hand—even if it took all night.

At the supper table, John moved his food around on his plate as though he could position it in a way that would make it more palatable. Even though his stomach was empty, food stuck in his throat as he nibbled absentmindedly.

"I'm sorry," Jeanne said. She looked like she was about to cry.

"Ah…don't mind me, dear. I'm havin' a hard time right now… 'n I know you are too." John reached over and patted Jeanne's hand that was curled into a tight ball. Death had created a heaviness between them that neither had the strength to dispel.

"I just need some answers, that's all," John said.

"We're gonna have to just recognize all of this as God's will." Jeanne said as she lifted her napkin to catch a tear that had escaped her eye.

"I don't know if I can accept that right now." John's voice grew more intense. "Do you really think it's God's will to kill all of our good church members?"

"Isn't that what the Bible says?" Now Jeanne's voice increased in volume. "It says that God giveth and God taketh away… doesn't it? You know how it was with Job."

"Is that what this is all about? Am I just a modern day Job destined to endure all kinds of disaster at the hands of God? What am I supposed to do? Curse God and die like Job's wife suggested. " John slammed his fork on the table. "To tell you the truth, Jeanne, maybe that's not such a bad idea after all. I don't think I like God very much right now."

Jeanne gasped then busted out crying. "Oh, John. Please don't say that," she sobbed. "We've got enough problems already without you talking bad about the Almighty."

"Well, I don't mean to talk bad about him or think bad about him either," John took a deep breath in an effort to calm himself down, "but if I'm gonna keep serving him, I need some answers 'cause I'm about ready to quit."

"Please John, please don't give up on God." Jeanne tugged on John's sleeve as he pushed his chair back from the table.

"Well, I've gone through the Old Testament and I've got no enlightenment yet. In fact, there is very little to put our hopes on there, what with the curse, 'n then there's all that death and destruction. I guess if it weren't for what Adam and Eve did we wouldn't be in the shape we're in now."

John stood up as though he was about to stomp out of the room. But seeing Jeanne so distressed, he slipped over behind her chair instead and wrapped his arms around her. Laying his cheek on the top of her head, he said. "I'm sorry. I shouldn't have upset you. No, I'm not gonna quit yet. But I will get some answers. I will…"

John gave her a quick hug and patted the top of her head. "Don't worry about me if I don't come to bed. I'm staying with the Bible 'til I find what I am lookin' for. Just pray…just pray…"

Back in his study, John plopped down at his desk once again. Carefully he opened his worn Bible. This time he turned the pages until he came to the New Testament. That's where he would continue his quest…

Part Two

Chapter Five

The Wilderness of Judea

As far as Yeshua could see, there was nothing in sight except barren hills of infertile limestone that stretched for miles upon end. Overhead, the sun blasted its scorching rays into the pulverized Senonian chalk that made up the vast expanse of the wilderness of Judah. Here and there were tiny patches of brownish-green vegetation courageously gripping the unfriendly soil, desperately trying to retain a spark of life in spite of the vicious beating from the Khamsin that had assaulted the whole region the day before.

Yesterday had been rough. From the first moment Yeshua had entered those barren hills, it had been a struggle. He had only walked a few laborious miles when the *Khamsin* had struck with very little warning. Every time this violent, hot, dry wind blew out of the east instead of its usual westerly direction from the Mediterranean Sea, the *Khamsin*, or *Sirocco* as it was called, would fill the air with a fine dust that permeated everything, causing extreme discomfort in humans and animals alike. Through its relentless battering, all the vegetation in its path was normally pounded into lifeless ruin.

Yeshua had pressed on for a time, bracing himself against the relentless gale. Tiny grains of sand had bombarded his face like angry missiles determined to tear into every pore of his exposed skin. Even with his girdle wrapped around his face, the gritty substance had found its way into his mouth, nose, and eyes. With every breath, he suspected he had been breathing pure dust instead of air. Finally, Yeshua had found a slight indention in the side of a rise and purposefully curled up and slept until the tempest had blown itself out.

Only a day had passed since that destructive event had left a trail of desolation in its route, sucking the life out of what little foliage had survived the beginning of the dry season. Yeshua leaned wearily on his crooked walking stick as he gazed on the formidable panorama of monotonous, barren mountains that lay ahead. Fine, gritty dust clung to his long, tangled hair, changing its appearance from dark and glossy to a dull, dingy shade. He paid very little attention to the gray powdery residue that covered his hands and feet and hardly noticed the gritty dust that also permeated his once clean robe. Clapping his hands together to shake off the worst of the grime and then giving his cloak a quick passing swipe, he sat down on the blistering sand, oblivious to the discomfort it presented.

When he had been drawn—or better yet, driven—into the wilderness by the Holy Spirit, he had no idea what to expect or why he was even being led here. He did know, however, without a doubt this was where he was to be. Already, he sensed it was not going to be a time of pleasure.

Whereas the day before had been filled with ferocious howling winds, today, as the sun arose in a cloudless sky, it was greeted with a welcome stillness that could almost be touched in its intensity. Yeshua leaned back on his elbows as he examined the cerulean sky overhead.

"Father, thank you for this beautiful day; this is the day you have made. I will rejoice and be glad in it." He swiped the back of his hand across his parched lips.

"I am so grateful for the refuge of your arms that sheltered me in the midst of the storm last night, but Father, I could really use a drink of water and a bath."

He looked around at the arid land envisioning a wash basin full of sparkling water resting on the desolate soil, inviting him in for a welcome refreshing bath. *As wonderful as my heavenly Father is,* he thought, *I don't think that is going to happen.* He chuckled to himself.

Yeshua pushed himself up from his uncomfortable resting place to a standing position and watched the sun begin its steady climb across the bright clear sky. *It's only going to get hotter,* he calculated.

His mouth felt like it was made of cotton except for the accumulation of grit that clung to his tongue. He spat what he could on the ground and then spoke out loud to the empty barrenness. "I have to find some water soon." He surveyed his surroundings with renewed determination.

When he had come into the wilderness, he had understood that he was not going to need food because his plan was to fast. For how long, he didn't know. Without food, he knew he could last as long as fifty days; but without water in this scorched region, dehydration would become a quick destroyer.

Glancing once again at the trajectory of the sun, Yeshua set his course eastward where he knew the Wadi Qilt was located that entered the Rift Valley near Jericho. There he hoped to find water. Even though very little rain fell on this bleak and barren wilderness area, to the west where Jerusalem was located, there was an abundance of precipitation during the rainy season. The Wadi Qilt served as a watershed during that time, allowing water to cascade into the Rift Valley where the Dead Sea was located.

Yeshua was hoping that if he could get to the Wadi Qilt, he would find a stream still flowing or some unpolluted pools of standing water, even though for the past month the land had been experiencing the beginning of the dry season. As he methodically trudged through the burning sand, he was startled by a lizard that darted across his path. The small, scaly creature raced to a patch of withered shrubbery probably looking for the hiding place of a bug or two.

A lizard was no problem, but Yeshua had heard stories of large lions lurking around the riverbeds just waiting for some unsuspecting prey to show up in this forsaken territory. Besides lions, he was aware that this wilderness was home to bears, leopards, and cheetahs, not to mention the various kinds of deadly snakes hiding in undetected dens. And even the onager, or wild ass as some people called them, was known to attack a man if they were desperate enough. For an unarmed person traveling through this desolate terrain, any one of these wild beasts could present a real threat.

But Yeshua was not afraid. He was about his Father's business—whatever that might be in this barren region. He loved people and enjoyed talking, laughing, and listening to them, but his most treasured time was when he had the opportunity to fellowship with his heavenly Father. Here in this forsaken wilderness, he would have ample time for undisturbed communion. But first he had to find water.

As he plodded through the hot desert sand, his mind replayed the events of the past few days. He had made his way from Nazareth in Galilee to the southern part of the Jordan River east of Jericho. There, his cousin John, who had been dubbed the Baptist, had been baptizing converts and declaring the kingdom of God. John had grown in popularity so much so that Jerusalem, all of Judea, and people from the country round about the Jordan area flocked to hear him, desiring to be baptized while they confessed their sins.

When news had reached Yeshua of John's appearance in the wilderness, he knew his time had come to begin the ministry his Father had commissioned him to do. He had poured over the Scriptures after his Father had made his mission clear and had discovered in the book of Isaiah that there would one day come one—a voice crying in the wilderness—to prepare the way for him.

When he had heard the reports of all that John was doing, he couldn't wait to go to the site where he was preaching. Something inside was compelling him to submit to the baptism of John. But when his cousin had seen him coming, even though this had been the first time they had seen each other since they had grown up, John had raised his voice and announced loudly: "Behold the Lamb of God that takes away the sins of the world! I baptize you with water unto repentance, but he who is coming after me is mightier than I, whose sandals I am not worthy to take off or even carry. He will baptize you with the Holy Spirit and with fire."

As Yeshua had gazed into the passionate eyes of this fiery preacher, he had been overcome with joy and love for this plain unsophisticated man—rough on the outside, but it had been obvious to Yeshua that at some time or other John had experienced a visitation from the heavenly Father. So far in his thirty years of life, Yeshua had not met another human being that had any grasp at all as to what his mission would be—except maybe his mother. And she only knew that he had a heavenly commission, but as to the details, well, this man definitely knew more than she did.

Yeshua had eagerly drawn John aside informing him that he wanted to be baptized. But John had protested strenuously, "No, no! Why do you come to me?" Astonished at the request, the Baptist insisted, "It is I who need to be baptized by you."

But Yeshua had been adamant. "You must do this. This is the fitting way for both of us to fulfill all righteousness. We must perform completely whatever is right."

Yeshua had had no idea just how pleasing that simple act of submission and obedience would be to the Father. For when he came up out of the water, it seemed as though the heavens had opened over their heads, and in that remarkable moment, all eyes beheld the Spirit of God descending upon him in the form of a dove.

But then the whole multitude stood riveted in awe as a thunderous voice resounded from heaven saying, "This is my Son, my beloved, in whom I delight!"

Many had fallen on their faces trembling in fear at the sound of that voice. Yeshua and John had stood enraptured with their hands lifted heavenward as pure, unadulterated love washed through their whole being.

It seemed that somehow that moment had been frozen in time, for how long, they had lost track. Finally, the sense of that heavenly presence had lifted enough that they could move. Even then, Yeshua and John had embraced each other with a sense of camaraderie that extended far beyond the natural realm and had united them spirit to spirit.

Yeshua was jerked back to the present as the unrelenting rays of the sun coiled its sweltering tentacles around the weary traveler. Still, he continued to press onward over one sand dune after another. Finally, when Yeshua felt he could not take another step, he crested the next hill and beheld at the bottom of a huge valley the magnificent Wadi Qilt spread out in a panoramic view. From where he stood, he could see the sun striking what appeared to be a thin stream of water at the bottom of the ravine.

Driven by an overpowering thirst, Yeshua scrambled down the closest trail to the bottom but in his haste lost his footing several times and very nearly plummeted down the incline head first. At last, after dropping to a grassy ledge, there underneath its lip, some three feet below, lay a beautiful pool of clear water.

It didn't take him long to vault those last three feet, landing at the outer edge of the water. He resisted the urge to emerge his whole body in the refreshing pond; instead, he knelt and gulped handfuls after handfuls of the thirst-quenching liquid. Only after he had enjoyed his fill did he splash water on his face and hands. He relished the pleasant sensation of clean skin for the first time since he had walked into this wilderness. It felt so good that he plunged his whole head beneath the surface and vigorously rinsed the grime from his hair.

As he started to strip off his loose outer garment to dry himself with, Yeshua halted, frozen in place with his robe half on and half off. There on the opposite side of the pool, crouching as though ready to pounce, sat a huge lion. Its lips were curled back in a snarl, revealing a mouthful of sharp, dangerous teeth that looked quite capable of ripping a man to shreds.

"Did I take over your watering hole, big fellow?" Yeshua asked softly. Carefully and deliberately, he continued to take off his cloak. All the while, he chatted with the lion in a soothing manner.

"There's enough water here for the both of us. Would you like to come join me? It is quite refreshing, you know." Then purposely, with calmness that radiated from confidence generated from the inside, not the outside, Yeshua held out his hand to the lion as though he intended to shake his paw.

For a moment, the lion looked confused, and then abruptly, he arose and padded silently to the water's edge opposite Yeshua.

"I think you and I could become great friends." Yeshua laughed quietly. "At least I wouldn't have to worry about you dominating the conversation."

Yeshua continued to dry his face and hair and then retreated into the shade under the grassy ledge. He found a cool, sandy spot and folded his cloak into a makeshift pillow and stretched out on the ground. Clasping his hands behind his head, he watched the lion drink his fill. Yeshua must have fallen asleep because the next thing he knew, or maybe sensed, was something moving close to his right arm. He carefully lifted his head to see what it was, and there beside him lay the lion. He was the picture of contentment. Positioned the way he was, he seemed to be making a statement: "I don't just want to be your friend; I will be your protector."

Yeshua rolled over on his side and stroked the large animal's fur. "I feel a little like Daniel." He said, looking around curiously, "I can't see you right now." Yeshua addressed the unseen being he felt sure was standing close by, "But I know the Father has sent an angel to watch over me. So thanks." With that, he decided the cloak was a poor excuse for a pillow so he leaned his head against the lion and drifted back to sleep.

Chapter Six

The sun had already made its appearance above the horizon, releasing its comforting warmth into the dry, morning air when Yeshua finally awoke. Yeshua had passed the night in peaceful sleep curled up next to Rayah the lion, drawing warmth from his body heat to stave off the night's chill. Before he had drifted into slumber, Yeshua had settled on the name Rayah for his newfound comrade. Already Rayah—meaning "friend"—had proved to be a trusty companion. Yeshua liked having someone to talk to in this lonely terrain even if his four-legged acquaintance could not answer back.

"Someone who doesn't talk back actually makes a perfect friend." Yeshua laughed to himself as he patted the large animal on his broad shoulder. Rayah stretched lazily at the sound of a human voice and pushed his muscular frame to a standing position. Gently nudging Yeshua with his massive head, he headed for the watering hole.

After drinking his fill, Rayah vigorously shook the water from his mane. With a long, backward look at Yeshua as though seeking his permission, he bounded away, easily mounting the ravine's edge as he disappeared from sight.

"I guess someone around here needs to eat," Yeshua acknowledged as he gave a quick good-bye nod to the lion. Kneeling by the refreshing pool of water, he busied himself with quenching his overnight thirst and doing what he could to prepare for another hot, sweltering day in the wilderness.

Yeshua surveyed his surroundings once again. After walking a short way in both directions from where he had spent the night, he determined that this area, with plenty of water and a ledge that jutted out over the ravine, would be a perfect place to spend his days in the wilderness. The shelf that protruded from the side of the narrow valley afforded a naturally shaded area to protect him from the sun's relentless rays. The sparse vegetation had been spared the scorching effects of the *Khamsin*, which gave this secluded spot the slight impression of a scantily decked-out garden area.

I think this is the perfect spot, Yeshua thought. Relieved that he could settle down and not go any farther, Yeshua found a comfortable site beside a large boulder and sat down.

First of all, he was planning on having a lengthy conversation with his heavenly Father. That was the part of the day that Yeshua always looked forward to the most. Those wonderful times of prayer had never been a one-way conversation. The strength and joy that came from hearing the voice of his Father had always been a source of pure delight. He was especially excited about today; Yeshua had been looking forward to conversing with his Father about the announcement that had resonated from heaven at his baptism. His heart warmed as he realized that Elohim had confirmed his mission in front of the whole world—assuming, of course, that the news would spread quickly like any other unusual occurrence was prone to do.

Once he got situated, Yeshua lifted his voice to the heavens. "Elohim, my Father, I don't know why I am here in this deserted place, but I know you have brought me here for a purpose. Thank you for the kind words you spoke about me before those many witnesses. I am grateful for the privilege to do your eternal work here on earth, and I am grateful for your spirit that invigorates and guides me continually. I have come, O Addoni, to do your will."

Pausing for a moment in his prayer, Yeshua listened intently for that still, small voice that in the past had never failed to respond. But for the first time since he could remember, he heard nothing. He waited and listened for a little while longer but still heard nothing. Yeshua continued.

"What is the next step in the plan you have for me? How do you want me to go about letting the world know how much you love them? I want to show them how your heart is broken because of their suffering. Because of sin, they are under such an oppressive load from the curse that has been imposed upon them from the adversary."

Again, Yeshua became quiet, allowing ample time for the Father to answer. All was as still as before. Far in the distance, the mournful cry of a bird pierced the air, having found a nesting place in a small cave along the limestone wall of the wadi, which had been hollowed out by an ancient cave dweller. A bush rustled now and then as a slight breeze found its way into the valley floor momentarily caressing its partially dried-out branches. But all else was silent.

A loneliness gripped Yeshua like he had never experienced before. The presence of his Father seemed to have faded sometime in the night. This was a new and frightening experience. Even as a small child, he had always been able to detect the presence of his heavenly Father no matter where he was. During his childhood, he had known he was different from his playmates in that respect. Because his heavenly Father had strictly charged him to keep quiet regarding the information that he, and only he, knew, Yeshua had never let on or bragged about what he had experienced. He had been told that there would come a time when the truth of who he really was could be released to the world.

Yeshua hadn't known automatically where he came from or who he was. He was like any other person born into the world with no prior knowledge. He didn't even remember a lot about his early childhood, except the things his mother had told him about the curious events that had accompanied his unusual birth. But one event that was forever etched in his mind happened when he was but five years old.

His memory of that day was remarkably vivid. His mother had had a busy day planned so she had taken him to his earthly father's carpenter shop, which was attached to the north side of their house. She presented him with a bucket of various sized wood scraps to play with and then went about preparing the evening meal in another part of the house. Because Joseph was out of town delivering a table that he had repaired, Yeshua had been all alone in the shop. Being alone had never been a problem for him. He loved to take the odd-shaped wood remnants and create imaginary houses and villages. There, surrounded by the pungent smell of freshly cut cedar and oak, he could entertain himself for hours.

That day, he had been playing for only a short time when suddenly, a bright cloud filled the room. At first, Yeshua was so startled that he couldn't move or cry out as the dazzling light overshadowed him. Then a voice, overflowing with peace and love, spoke to him. Right away Yeshua's young heart was calmed. Quietly, he listened while he had his first conversation with his heavenly Father.

That day, Elohim had told Yeshua who he really was, making clear that he was in fact the Son of God. His heavenly Father had then explained that Yeshua was indeed the Messiah that had been foretold by the prophets, letting him know that even though Joseph had stepped in to become his earthly father, that he, Elohim, was actually his real Father.

Afterward, Elohim had communicated to Yeshua some highlights concerning his earthly mission that was to take place many years later, and then the cloud had lifted. Once again, Yeshua was alone.

That had been a momentous revelation for a young child to comprehend, but even at five years of age, Yeshua had always seemed to be wiser and more mature than his peers. Oh, sure, he had had fun with them, but after that remarkable visitation, he had felt even more detached than ever from their childish world.

Even his mother had seen a difference in him after that, especially when they had made that eventful trip to Jerusalem for the Passover feast. While there, he had felt compelled to seek out the rabbis in the court of the temple, determined to listen to and ask questions of them. There was so much he didn't know about what the Scriptures said about the Messiah. He had been tenacious in his quest to find out as much as he could from those who had spent years pouring over the ancient texts. Time had passed so swiftly that he had been amazed to realize that his parents had left town without him and finally come back looking for him.

His mother scolded him for treating them with such disregard. Yeshua had apologized for causing them distress, but he had been surprised that they—or at least, his mother—had not figured out how necessary it had been that he be in his Father's house, occupied about his Father's business. However, after that incident, because he loved them so deeply, he had been careful to strictly obey his parents so he would not be the cause of any more undue pain.

As Yeshua reflected on that childhood visitation, once again, he mulled over everything he had read from the holy Scriptures along with what his Father had told him about his mission. His mission! Here in this Judean wilderness, Yeshua had been expecting his Father to fill in all the details that he still did not know, but so far, he had heard nothing. Oh, well, it had been only one day. He would give his heavenly Father as much time as he needed. He wasn't going anywhere, and so far, he had had no hunger pangs. So he spent the rest of the day singing psalms to the Father he adored and enjoying the solitude of his makeshift sanctuary.

That evening, Rayah did not return to keep him company. Yeshua was a little disappointed considering how his day had gone. He was feeling a little lonely. *Having company—even the four-legged kind—would be nice,* he thought. As the night wrapped its oppressive cloak of darkness around Yeshua, he finally fell into a fitful sleep.

But even in his sleep, he was disturbed by strange dreams. He dreamed that he was in the midst of a flaming inferno with no way out. The flames were licking at his hair and clothing while grotesque and misshapen beings taunted him with malicious laughter, chanting in a sadistic, guttural chorus: "Who do you think you are? You are nobody. You can't even get out of here alive."

In the dream, Yeshua screamed out for his heavenly Father to rescue him from the flames, but his pleas were met with stone silence. Finally, in despair, Yeshua crumbled to his knees as the flames completely enveloped him.

Yeshua awoke with a start. He jerked upright with sweat bathing his trembling body. Where was he? What was he doing here? In the faint light of dawn, he could just make out the water hole. He sat down once again and tried to calm down by praying. It helped, but still, there was no answer, nor was there any sense of the peaceful presence of his heavenly Father.

Yeshua was confused. Why was this happening to him? Maybe he had gotten out of the will of Elohim after all. Was he really the Messiah, the hope of the world? Right then, he certainly didn't feel like it.

After washing in the pool and going about his morning ritual, Yeshua began to feel more normal. The horror of the night faded as the sun peeked over the edge of the wadi wall, bathing the valley with its golden glow. Even though Elohim had not revealed himself to Yeshua, still he prayed. He prayed and prayed. He sang every psalm he had memorized from rabbinical school and then made up some of his own. Finally as the day wore on, he sat propped against the wadi wall and meditated on all the scriptures he could remember that had been written about the Messiah.

As he filled his mind with the comforting written words of his Father, once again, peace and assurance flooded his troubled soul. Even if he had not been able to detect the *voice* of his Father, still, he had his *words* buried deep in his heart, and they could not be taken away.

☼ Chapter Seven

Yeshua's third night in the wilderness was less eventful than the one before. He slept the night through much more peacefully without interruption and was startled to be awakened by the moist nose of Rayah rubbing against his beard. When he realized what had awakened him, he was delighted that his friend was back. He sat up, massaged the sleep out of his eyes, and ran his fingers through the thick tangle of Rayah's mane.

"You decided to come back, did you? Well, ole boy, did you have a good hunt?" Yeshua playfully patted Rayah's belly as he stretched out on his back at Yeshua's side.

"Feels like your tummy is plenty full. Maybe you'll keep me company for a little longer this time. By the way, where were you when I needed you? I sure could have used your company yesterday." Yeshua gave the large animal a good-natured shove and headed for the water hole.

Man and beast splashed around in the cool, refreshing water for a while and found a smooth, rocky slab on the sunny side of the valley where they stretched out to dry off in the warmth of the morning sun. Rayah promptly fell asleep. Yeshua stared contentedly at the cloudless sky allowing his eyes to follow the lazy pattern of a hawk gliding far above the top of the wadi's wall.

"Father, the heavens declare your glory, and the firmament shows and proclaims your handiwork. I greatly rejoice in you, O Addoni, for you send blessings of good things to meet me. I trust and am confident in you, for you make me to be blessed and a blessing forever."

Yeshua heard no answering voice as his prayer of thanksgiving ascended heavenward, but today, it didn't seem to matter. The very presence of Elohim's words in his mouth and heart was enough.

The steady breathing of the great beast sleeping beside Yeshua was both soothing and reassuring, reminding him of the goodness and care of his heavenly Father. Once again, he took advantage of the stillness and solitude of the day to reflect on the special times he had spent with his heavenly Father.

• • • • • • • • • • • • • • • • • • • •

Several years after he had first heard the voice of Elohim at five years old, it had happened again when he had just reached manhood. But this time, it was marvelously different; it had occurred one night when everyone in the household was fast asleep except for him. Off and on all day long, he had experienced an unusual sense of excitement and expectancy. When he finally crawled into bed that night, he had trouble falling asleep. He was lying there praying when all at once he saw a blinding flash of light. There, standing at the foot of his bed, was a magnificent being clothed in dazzling white garments. His form was similar to that of a man only taller than any Yeshua had ever seen before. His face and countenance emitted a heavenly light.

"Most holy one," the angel announced reverently, "you have an appointment with El Elyon. I have come to escort you to his throne."

With that, he bowed deeply then guided Yeshua out the door where a splendid chariot sat, which almost seemed to be made of light. Its appearance looked as if it were covered with pure, transparent gold, elaborately adorned with ornamentation far surpassing the finest Roman designs. The chariot was completely enclosed round about with something like windows; no horses were connected to power it.

At the angel's bidding, Yeshua had seated himself on the lavish, velvety upholstery that made up the interior of the heavenly coach. The chariot began to rise without a sound at an indescribable rate of speed. The earth with its cities, towns, and mountains vanished in the distance. Soon, it seemed that the moon was beneath their feet as they sped through the heavens. Stars could be seen everywhere as Yeshua and the angel were propelled throughout the regions of the solar system, leaving Yeshua's earthly place of birth behind while fast approaching his real place of origin.

Soon, the brilliant lights of a city clothed in splendor and radiance came into view surrounded by towering walls, their luster resembling rare and precious jewels like jasper shining as clear as crystal. Yeshua could see that the city had foundations garnished with all manner of precious stones. Twelve foundations sparkled with sapphire, emeralds, topaz, amethyst, diamonds, and other brilliant jewels presenting the appearance of a majestic stairway. Embedded in the city walls, three on each side, were twelve massive gates with frames and hinges of the purest gold, each made of one colossal pearl.

Quickly, they covered the distance to the city, passing through an exquisite valley where on each side of the foothills stood forests of symmetrical trees unlike anything he had seen on the earth. Each tree was tall and graceful, perfect and unblemished without any brown spots or dead leaves anywhere. The valley floor was stunning with elegant grass, each blade perfect and erect, intermingled with brilliant white flowers touched with a splash of gold at their centers. The valley was hemmed in by majestic mountains interspersed with lively streams of sparkling water. Flowers in every color of blue, yellow, red, purple, all shades of amber, and gold that were transparent like crystal decorated the verdant meadows that led into the valley.

As the chariot approached the Judean gate, Yeshua noticed a huge angel stationed just outside equipped with a large, daunting sword. Just as they were slowing down to go through the gate, the sentinel angel stepped forward to welcome them into the city. Upon seeing the passenger in the chariot, he halted in amazement and instantly fell prostrate to the ground. With a loud voice, he shouted, "Hallelujah! Blessing and glory, majesty, power, and might be ascribed to Jehovah Elohim and to the Lamb who is to redeem mankind throughout the ages and ages forever and ever, throughout the eternities of the eternities!"

Voice after voice took up that refrain until it seemed that all of heaven reverberated with the mighty anthem of the Lamb. From every corner of the celestial city came the thunderous shout of a great crowd of heavenly beings exclaiming, "Hallelujah! Praise Jehovah Elohim. Salvation and glory, splendor, majesty and power, dominion and authority belong to the Lamb of God!"

The angel who had been driving the chariot also bowed his head while praises continued to fill the heavenly atmosphere within the golden city. A moment passed, and then he lifted his hand and said, "We must proceed to the throne of Elohim; Jehovah doth await thee."

Slowly, they glided down the broadway in the middle of the city. A river that sparkled like crystal flowed along the side of the boulevard, which appeared to be coming from the direction of Jehovah's throne. On either side of the river were trees of life with twelve varieties of fruit. The angel mentioned that these trees yielded a fresh crop of fruit each month.

Nowhere to be seen was anything that could defile or contaminate the purity and holiness of that heavenly realm. As Yeshua drew nearer to the magnificent throne, so stately that it could be seen from every direction, he could hear the sound of an ensemble of trumpets heralding their imminent approach.

The floor around the throne looked like marble with veins of gold threads running throughout. Gushing from under the base of the throne was the River of Life, flowing in beauty and purity. Around and above the throne arched a rainbow in appearance like an emerald; its brilliant hues mixed with light produced intense, dazzling colors. Beneath the circle of this rainbow was the seat of the almighty Father. The grandeur and majesty of it was indescribable. It appeared to be upholstered with dazzling glory bathing everything with the shimmering colors of the rainbow. All the governing power of the universe issued from this throne.

Surrounding the throne was a myriad of angels that numbered ten thousand times ten thousand and thousands of thousands. Flying around the throne room were several big angels with wingspans of thirty feet or more who circled the throne singing and shouting, "The great God Jehovah!"

They cried, "Holy! Holy! Holy!" as they discovered fresh revelations of God's love and glory that they had never seen before. But when they caught sight of Yeshua making his way to the throne, they ceased flying, folded their wings, and bowed reverently.

As Yeshua approached the huge platform that encompassed the throne, waves of light and glory rolled over him, bathing him with a refreshing wash of love, peace, and joy. Clouds of glistening light pulsated from the being shrouded behind a brilliant veil. Then out from the miasma of radiant splendor came a voice like the sound of great waters and like the rumbling of mighty thunder; yet it was as melodious as the music of harpists stroking their instruments.

"Come up hither, my son," the voice commanded.

Yeshua deliberately ascended the steps leading to the throne. Boldly, he stepped into the massive pulsating cloud of energy and light. For the first time since becoming a flesh and blood man, he faced his heavenly Father.

And there in that cathedral of glory, Father and Son, with hearts beating together as one, embraced with a pure love known only in the celestial realm. A love united in such harmony that it overflowed throughout heaven, sending waves of glory all over the universe, ultimately invading the darkness of planet earth with rays of hope and expectancy.

In that tender moment, Jehovah Elohim addressed his beloved son, "Yeshua, you are man as well as God—for you have been born of a woman. All power and authority shall soon be given into your hands, and you shall lay down your life for the salvation of men. You were known as the Word before your incarnation, but now you shall be called the Son of Man."

Then as night wore on in the earth, the heavenly Father unfolded in panoramic detail events that took Yeshua back through the corridors of time—before time had yet begun; even before the foundations of the earth.

Chapter Eight

As Yeshua continued to recall that eventful night some fifteen years before, he remembered it had all been somewhat overwhelming to his young mind, but as he had stood in the presence of the Creator of the universe, it seemed right and somehow vaguely familiar. In fact, as Elohim unfolded the events of ages past, Yeshua's subconscious memory had been strangely stirred.

"My Son." El Elyon addressed Yeshua with all the tender love of a beloved Father who adores his only child. "I have brought you here to unveil the divine mysteries of certain things that have been hidden from you since you left this region of eternity to become man."

With a wave of the Father's hand, a surge of energy exploded into millions of light crystals that formed a panoramic picture screen on the canopy of radiance that engulfed the throne room. Gradually images began to take shape. Yeshua detected the form of three beings standing together as though in intense conversation. As he looked closer, he could distinguish the features of the one standing in the middle. The resemblance was unmistakable. There, he, Yeshua, stood more mature, and in a celestial form in the timeless past, but without doubt, he had been there.

"You do not remember, my Son, what came to pass before the foundations of the earth, but you had a key part in the plans and renovation of planet earth. Before there ever was a tree or river or even a creature formed, you willingly agreed to become a lamb slain to atone for the sins of all mankind. This was going to be necessary in order to redeem them from the control of an evil ruler, even though, at that time, mankind had not yet been created. However, my Son, evil did exist."

Then on the brilliant celestial screen appeared a marvelous creature, angelic in form and exceedingly beautiful, more dazzling than any other created being. He was covered with garments that had the appearance of shimmering gold, studded throughout with every kind of precious stone. When he moved, an aurora of luminosity sent out streamers and arches of colored lights that accompanied him wherever he went throughout heaven.

Pointing to the image on the screen, the Father explained, "That is Lucifer—Morning Star or the Shining One, as he was called by the angels who revered him. He was one of our three ruling archangels in the heavenly kingdom." At the mention of that name, fire arose in Jehovah's eyes with an intensity born from righteous wrath.

When Jehovah continued, however, his fierce countenance changed to sadness. "Lucifer had been created with the remarkable ability to inspire and influence others through stirring melodious worship and was noted for his exceptional musical compositions that were sung all over heaven. But iniquity was found in him. He allowed pride to germinate in his heart, and consequently, he became lifted up because of his beauty. Aspiring to supremacy and coveting honor and glory beyond his rank, he began to sow a spirit of deception and discontentment among the angels that were under his command. Before long, that discontentment blossomed into open revolt."

Then in living action, Yeshua witnessed the drama that had unfolded in ages past when war had broken out in heaven. There on that heavenly screen, once again, Yeshua beheld in his incarnate human body what he had witnessed long ago in his heavenly form: he beheld Lucifer, who became Satan, fall like lightning from heaven to invade the earth with his evil, wicked influence.

Deeply moved by what he had just seen, Yeshua stood motionless, letting the impact of what he had observed sink in. Then his Father interrupted his thoughts as he continued. "When the decision had been made to renovate earth and create the new creature called man that would rule and take dominion over the earth, we were aware that a strong, formidable, power-hungry enemy who was already ravaging the earth would ultimately contend for that authority. Satan had become determined to rule. We knew he could not be satisfied to allow any other being to gain control over any of his domain."

Jehovah then turned to Yeshua. "Because we gave mankind a free will just as the angels have, there was a certainty that Satan would use it to try to gain control of the earth once again. That is why we had to have a plan in place should man make the wrong choice."

"Why, Father," Yeshua asked respectfully, "did you give your created man a free will, when there would be such a great danger that he would willingly hand the earth's authority over to Satan?"

"Well, my Son," Jehovah explained, obviously pleased with Yeshua's desire to understand. "For any creature to be capable of ruling and reigning, one must have intelligence. Therefore, to have intelligence, one must have a free will; otherwise, he could not make the required decisions to effectively rule."

Yeshua glanced once more at the images displayed before him. "It must have been especially important that you gain dominion over planet earth, or you would not have taken the risk to create such a man."

"Yes." The heavenly Father continued. "It was of the greatest consequence. For as righteous rulers of the universe, we could not allow evil to dominate even one area of the cosmos."

Jehovah stopped as an image of the earth appeared on the screen surrounded by an innumerable company of sinister beings. All Yeshua could see was a planet engulfed in utter darkness without form and completely void of light and life.

"When we created man out of the dust of the earth, we established his right to legally live and function there. But in the process, he was required to guard and protect the earthly environment from the influence of Satan. That responsibility, in itself, was impossible for them to carry out without the wisdom and heavenly anointing that they would receive from the divine life that was breathed into them when they were created. Because they were earthborn and not gods—even though they were made in our image—they were totally dependent on the knowledge and ability they would receive from a divine source."

Jehovah hesitated momentarily as though he was revisiting the emotions resurrected by the tragic consequences of Adam's disobedience. Then he continued. "Since Satan was a spirit being and had ingenuity and knowledge that he had retained from his time in heaven, he could lord it over an earthbound creature. However, one with a vital connection to the wisdom that came from heaven was greater in every way than the evil one that would seek to rule the earth. Therefore, it was imperative that mankind strictly obey my commands and gain their knowledge from me in order to carry out the commission to rule in the earth."

Then the scene changed, and Yeshua saw the beautiful paradise garden on earth where everything was perfect and delightful. Adam and Eve, the dearly loved creation of Elohim, were going about their blissful routine with confidence, contentment, and pleasure.

"Their liberties were unbounded in the garden, and they should have been content," Jehovah explained. "I had warned them that the consequences of eating from the tree of the knowledge of good and evil would be death."

Yeshua watched in dismay as their ancient enemy of righteousness entered the body of a serpent and proceeded to seduce, deceive, and tempt the first couple to disobey the command of God. His heart broke as Adam and Eve finally succumbed, and then he wept openly at the penalties that followed—the shame, disgrace, and alienation from God.

Systematically, the ensuing events unfolded before Yeshua's sorrowful eyes: the sentence, the curse on the ground, and the banishment of Adam and Eve from the garden.

"Why, Addoni, was that tree placed in the garden at all?" Yeshua asked as tears continued to gather in his eyes.

"Righteous law demanded that anyone who is given unlimited authority pass the test of obedience. Lucifer failed that test, and judgment fell upon him. Mankind had to pass it in order to escape the same sentence pronounced on the angels of disobedience. When they failed, however, we already had a plan in place to save them from judgment and reestablish their authority.

Once again, they turned back to the drama unfolding from the beginning of time. It was obvious that Adam and Eve had been reluctant to leave the garden; consequently, two angels came with scourges in hand to force them out lest they eat of the tree of life and live forever in that pitiful state.

Even though the entire garden was charged and filled with the aroma of the tree of life and the atmosphere was surcharged with life, death was creeping upon Adam and Eve with the chill and shroud of its terrible blow. Obviously, they were out of harmony with that glorious environment having lost their covering of glory. The curse of death was upon them, and as a result, Jehovah had to send them out to till the ground, which he had likewise cursed.

"But through all of this, I showed them mercy and kindness, giving to them the promise of a redeemer," Elyon said as he drew Yeshua close and looked fully into his eyes with profound compassion. "You, my Son, are that redeemer. You must gain back what Satan has stolen. And even though you are my only begotten Son, you too must pass the test."

Yeshua leaned his head upon the breast of El Elyon as he breathed in life and strength from his nearness, struggling to comprehend the full extent of what he had just seen and heard. Enfolded there in his father's embrace, he felt the heartbeat and emotions of his Abba Father that clearly indicated, "I know what is ahead for you, and I do not want to let you go."

Once again, Yeshua lifted his eyes to the vision before him; there he observed the proof of the love Jehovah had for his fallen creation. He beheld the garments that Adam and Eve had been given to cover their shame—coverings that had been made from the innocent lamb that he himself had sacrificed.

That first lamb had given his life to cover the sins of Adam and Eve, but Yeshua knew that lamb was only a type and shadow of that which was to come. He, Yeshua, would give his life, not just to cover sins, but to once and for all cleanse hearts from the ravages of sin and completely purify any that would accept his sacrifice from all guilt and condemnation. And for those thus justified from sin's dominion, they would once again receive the authority to rule and reign over Satan and his kingdom as God had intended in the beginning.

• •

Lying there on the rock in the Judean wilderness, with Rayah still sleeping soundly beside him, Yeshua once again relived the anguish and pain and also the victory and triumph of that surreal moment. He recalled the beloved face of his Father as he had seen it that night. A countenance radiating pure light, complete with all the divine attributes of love, goodness, mercy, power, wisdom, and knowledge, all revealed in sweet harmony.

As he recalled those precious moments, strong waves of longing washed over him as he lifted his eyes to the blue canopy overhead that separated earth from the glorious land from which it originated. Tears bathed his face as he thought of the horrible consequences that sin and the curse had wrought in the earth that was now his home. The intense love that his heavenly Father had for mankind completely overwhelmed his heart and, yes, even threatened to break it into pieces with its heavy load of compassion.

Yeshua cried out from the depths of his heart, "Addoni, I willingly give you my life. My heart is broken for Adam's race. Here am I, oh, Lord, I am eager to become the Lamb, to lay down my life to take away the sins of the world."

Chapter Nine

Days passed in quick succession as Yeshua spent his time praying and meditating on the scriptures that had burned their message deep into his heart. On a few occasions, he and Rayah had taken short trips up and down the wadi just to pass the hours and enjoy the quiet solitude of their sanctuary. Some nights, Rayah would bound off in pursuit of wilderness game, but he always returned—sometimes only hours later, and occasionally, it would be a day or two before Yeshua would see him again. But Rayah always came back, showing signs that he missed his man-friend as much as Yeshua had missed his four-legged companion.

Yeshua lost track of how long he had been in the wilderness. He knew it had been well over two weeks since he had left the complexity of civilization to follow the leading of the Holy Spirit. Yeshua was thankful for the Spirit's leading and for the physical and spiritual strength he felt from his presence. But something unusual had happened that day when the dove had descended on him at his baptism. The Spirit that had always stirred so freely inside even from his earliest memories, that day, had come upon him in a measure that was almost tangible.

He sensed a power flowing inside that was not of this world. It was as though nothing would be impossible for him to do if he knew his heavenly Father had commanded him to do it. While he walked around and meditated on who he was and what he knew his mission was to be, sometimes he felt in a hurry to be about his Father's business. But Yeshua knew he could do nothing except what the Father directed him to do, so he was content to stay in that solitary place until he was released to step into his place of ministry.

He already had some indication of just how extensive and costly that ministry might be. On another occasion—eight years before, when he was twenty-two years of age—he had experienced one other visitation from Elohim.

• • • • • • • • • • • • • • • • • • • •

That particular morning, Yeshua kept feeling a compelling urge to pray, but it seemed the carpenter's shop had been busier than usual with people coming and going all day long. He had helped Joseph most of the day, but when it came time to close for the night, that longing to get alone with his heavenly Father persisted. So Yeshua had asked if it would be all right to take a long walk before the evening meal. Joseph had been more than happy to give Yeshua some much needed quiet time and suggested he take his evening meal along with him so he could stay longer. Yeshua's earthly father was always like that. Very seldom asking questions and always respectful of Yeshua's wishes as though there was an unspoken understanding between the two.

After grabbing a morsel of food and a jug of water, Yeshua headed for a small mountain some distance from Nazareth. With the sun still high in the early evening sky, Yeshua knelt by a large boulder to pray. Immediately, he began to sense heavenly beings all around, although he couldn't see them with his physical eyes. Many times in his life, he had known angels had been present in the room with him, and on rare occasions, they had even been momentarily visible. Always when this had happened, he had experienced a strong sense of peace and comfort, being made fully aware that the hosts of heaven were watching over him.

Yeshua had not been praying long that evening when he was startled to hear the sound of rushing wind as though a hurricane was approaching; however, not a leaf stirred nor a hair on his head moved. Astonished, he looked up, and there standing not over fifteen feet in front of him was a great pillar of fire—or at least it looked like fire. Even though it pulsated with energy, nothing on the ground was being consumed. The whole area round about was blanketed with a thick cloud like the smoke that ascends from a furnace.

Then out of the midst of the fire, Yeshua heard a voice. Right away, he recognized it as the voice of his heavenly Father—no one could mistake that voice. When Jehovah spoke, it seemed that all creation stood in attention at its authority.

"I have come to show you things that must shortly come to pass," he announced.

With that, a convincing manifestation of the presence of El Elyon stepped out from the midst of the blazing miasma. Yeshua found himself prostrate before Jehovah once again. The joy that filled his heart was overwhelming as he uttered genuine praise that poured like a river from the heart of the Son to his heavenly Father.

"Arise, my Son," Jehovah insisted, "for I have much to tell you."

As Yeshua slowly arose to his feet, heavenly glory bathed Father and Son for a space of time while flesh and spirit communed together about events that were to forever change the history of mankind and impact eternity without end.

"As you know," began Jehovah, "we created man to be upright and righteous. In the beginning, mankind possessed divine life. Even though he was made from the earth, he was created in our image and could hold communion with all that is divine as well as interact with the physical universe. Although he was material and possessed an animal nature, yet he was intellectual, moral, and pure, and a holy being, but still he rebelled and sin was born on earth."

Yeshua could not help but notice the sorrow with which his heavenly Father recounted those ancient happenings.

"When Adam and Eve fell," Jehovah continued, "the glory departed and their guilt alienated them from divine fellowship and divine life. As a result, the first pair became sinful; so the stream of humanity was contaminated at its source. Their descendants who were born in their image thus were fallen and depraved. Sin entered into the world because of one man, and death came as a result of sin, so sin passed upon all men. Because the stream of humanity became polluted at the fountainhead, this depravity became universal. The faculties and powers of the soul and body of mankind were then brought under the power of the evil one."

"Yes, Father, I have witnessed some of the horrors Satan has caused through wicked men," Yeshua said as he recalled the time a legion of Roman soldiers had stormed into Nazareth snatching up an unsuspecting rabbi named Symeon. After beating him mercilessly, they had nailed his hands and feet to the side of his own house amid his cries of excruciating pain. Yeshua never found out what the rabbi had done to deserve such treatment, but he did remember that even though Symeon's grieving family had taken him down and tried to nurse him the best they could, he had died the next day.

"It is true," said Jehovah. "Sin has spawned awful degradation on the earth. That is why not long after the fall of man, I decreed the law to Moses and the children of Israel. If anyone could have kept those laws perfectly, they would not have been under the control of the enemy. But no one could. The nature of sin was imbedded too deeply in the hearts of man. They were incapable of keeping the law."

"If mankind was not capable of keeping the law, then why give it to them at all?" questioned Yeshua.

"I gave the law so they would know what was right and what was wrong in my eyes. Without the law, they would have never known how sinful they really were. The first step to righteousness has always been for an individual to recognize his unrighteous condition. Once he acknowledges his sinfulness, then he realizes he cannot help himself."

"But there is hope, Father. You did make a way for the sins of mankind to be covered," Yeshua offered quickly.

"Yes, yes. That was our plan all along. The blood of an innocent life poured on the altar of sacrifice for the guilty. That was the only legal way for sin's atonement. Those sacrifices offered year after year could never make perfect those who approached the altars by cleansing and taking away their guilt or consciousness of sin. But as it is, those annual sacrifices brought a fresh remembrance of sins to be atoned for because the blood of bulls and goats is powerless to take away sins. You, my Son, have been thoroughly schooled in all of the laws pertaining to the sacrifices of bulls and goats, but those laws were merely a rude outline of the good things which are to come."

"Those good things which are to come are what I was born into this earth to bring about. Is that not true, Adoni?" Yeshua inquired thoughtfully.

"Yes, my Son, you are the hope of the world. Indeed, you have come to make possible reconciliation between God and man. Your life and your death, will secure a complete redemption and an everlasting release from Satan's clutches as your blood purifies the consciences of men from dead works and lifeless observances so that they can serve me, the ever-living God, once again instead of our enemy."

"So I did not come just to live on this earth. I came to die?"

"I am sorry to say there is no other way for the plan to work. Your life will reveal to mankind my everlasting love and the broad spectrum of my will, but your death will establish a new covenant so that all who accept your sacrifice might receive the fulfillment of the promised everlasting inheritance. Your death will open up a new and living way for fallen humanity and redeem them from the transgressions committed under the old covenant."

As Jehovah made that last sobering pronouncement, Yeshua stood for a brief moment while the full meaning of what he had heard began to sink in. Neither the Son of man nor the God of mankind spoke. Finally, Yeshua purposely and determinedly knelt in submission once again before El Elyon. Then in a voice trembling with emotion, Yeshua resolved, "Lo, here I am. Come to do your will, O Jehovah, to fulfill what is written of me in the volume of the Book. My Father, you have prepared a body for me to offer; I offer it to you freely."

"I know you are willing and obedient, my Son," Jehovah acknowledged with great sorrow. "But I warn you; it will not be easy. You will be rejected and forsaken by men. The very ones you have come to save will scorn you and will not appreciate your worth. You will be afflicted, and the judgment of mankind will fall upon you. You will be wounded for transgressions and bruised for iniquities, scourged so that people can be healed and made whole. Then finally, you will be betrayed and cruelly cruci-fied on a cross with the consent of the religious leaders, ridiculed by your people, and tormented by ruthless Roman soldiers."

Yeshua looked up at his loving Father, and then with tears streaming down his face, asked, "But will there be some that will not reject me, even one person who will be redeemed by my sacrifice?"

As he asked that question, Yeshua arose from his knees, then wiping his tears with the sleeve of his robe, he looked intently into the face of Jehovah. With fire in his eyes and great convic-tion in his voice, he stretched out his hands in the Father's direc-tion. "If there is only one person who is rescued from the hands of the enemy, then any suffering I must endure will be worth it."

"Oh, no, my Son, not just one will be saved," Jehovah replied, engulfing Yeshua with his massive loving arms. "But countless multitudes throughout the remainder of this age will not only receive deliverance from sin's dominion but will also rise up in the authority of your name and reign in life through your gift of righteousness. Satan will be put under their feet, and the gates of hell will not prevail over them."

Then placing both hands on Yeshua's shoulders, Jehovah con-tinued with such triumph in his eyes that Yeshua's body began to shake. "But in the end, death will be swallowed up in victory.

Even in the grave there will be triumph because its sting will be removed. The sting of death is sin, and the strength of sin is the law. Through your sacrifice, my Son, the penalty for sin will be paid, and the law will be fulfilled. Once that is done, your corruptible body will put on an incorruptible one, and you will rise triumphant."

As the mighty Elohim made that last victorious pronouncement, he laid his hands on Yeshua's head in a tender blessing. In the distance, a ram's horn sounded as though calling troops into battle, and the next thing Yeshua knew, he was once again alone on the mountainside.

Yeshua had lain there prostrate on that mountainside until the last rays of sun disappeared behind the crest of the mountain, and the night shadows deepened into the dark curtain of night. Crickets chirped their lullabies in the cool evening air, and the night owls began their hooting refrain as they announced the beginning of their nightly hunt. Still Yeshua did not move. The sobering information he had heard had drained him of strength but not resolve. The appearance of his heavenly Father had empowered his inner man. But he had already found that it was the outer man that always presented the problem.

So he was going to have to suffer the awful agonies of crucifixion. He had never actually seen anyone on a cross, but he had often heard described the awful details of that kind of atrocious punishment at the hands of the Romans. After witnessing the brutal torture of Symeon, it was hard to imagine the pain and suffering a human body would have to go through to experience that kind of a death.

●●●●●●●●●●●●●●●●●●●

As Yeshua continued to pace up and down the wadi floor, the remembrance of that solemn encounter with his heavenly Father filled his heart with delight, yet down deep lurked an overwhelming dread of what he knew lay ahead. There was no doubt in

Yeshua's mind that he could get through it. If it meant the works of the devil would be destroyed, then so be it. Yeshua was more than willing to endure whatever might come because of the joy that was set before him on the other side of the cross. If the burden of sin and the curse that it had brought on the human race could be lifted from even one person, it would be worth it.

Chapter Ten

As the evening drew to a close, Yeshua prepared for another night in the wilderness. Time had passed quickly, and any hunger pangs he had experienced early on had diminished almost completely by the third week. He had established a sort of routine, which included walking a short distance each day to exercise his physical body and then preparing his mind by recalling any scriptures he had learned. After singing and praying for hours each day, his spirit grew so strong that he found himself eager to leave the desert so he could demonstrate the love of his heavenly Father to the bewildered, harassed, and distressed multitudes.

However now was not the time to leave. He felt something more needed to be done here, but looking around at his pleasant hideaway, Yeshua had trouble understanding why this seclusion was even necessary. Yet he had learned there was always an important and eternal reason for everything the Father did. Yeshua would do nothing until he had the go-ahead from Jehovah.

All of a sudden, his thoughts were interrupted when he detected a movement out of the corner of his eye. He whirled around, and there positioned on the overhead ledge was Rayah. He had been gone longer than usual this time, and Yeshua had almost decided he might never see him again. Yet there he sat, having appeared as silently as a phantom. Even though Rayah remained perfectly motionless, something was different about him. His head was poised at an alert angle with eyes darting along the opposite crest of the wadi wall as though sensing something he could not see.

Yeshua took a step in Rayah's direction. "Welcome back, my friend. I have missed your company. Have you been visiting your family somewhere?" Then he stopped abruptly.

At the sound of Yeshua's voice, Rayah moved his head slightly but did not acknowledge Yeshua or take his eyes off the top of the wall.

"What is it, boy? Is something out there?" Yeshua turned to look at the spot where Rayah's attention was drawn. Nothing was there—at least nothing he could see, but Yeshua felt the hair on the nap of his neck raise as he began to sense a menacing presence. He couldn't see anything, but there was definitely something or someone up there.

Eerie shadows filled the valley floor as though a cloud had covered the sun, yet overhead, there was not a cloud in the sky. Yeshua was just trying to decide whether to go up top to take a look around when from the southern edge of the wadi, he heard a dreadful roar pierce the air with a reverberation so fierce that the rocks embedded in the wadi wall appeared to shake. The sound was like the fearsome call of a vicious hunter seeking something to devour. As Yeshua searched the wall in the direction from which the sound came, all of a sudden, he saw something. There, pacing back and forth at the peak of the ridge was the chilling silhouette of an enormous lion. His mane was as black as coal, not russet like Rayah's, and his razor-sharp fangs flashed from a snarl that looked alarmingly sinister.

Even from a distance, Yeshua could tell that this was no ordinary lion. Its evil intent was obvious by the way it threw his head and the purposeful way it paced back and forth. Its wiry, black tuft on the end of his tail swayed from side to side, taunting as though toying with its intended victim.

Yeshua stood motionless while a low growl rumbled in Rayah's throat. "Don't worry, Rayah; everything is going to be all right. He can't harm us." Yeshua spoke with a lot more confidence than he felt at the moment.

Now would be a really good time for an angel to show up, Yeshua thought.

For some reason, he felt more vulnerable than he had ever felt before. Inside, Yeshua was convinced that no evil could befall him, yet the very presence of the roaring lion had charged the atmosphere with such fear that it felt like an oppressive cloak threatening to overpower him.

As though sensing Yeshua's vulnerability, Rayah leapt from the ledge where he had been sitting and let out a deafening roar of his own, positioning himself between Yeshua and the renegade lion. With his tail swishing back and forth, Rayah dropped to a crouching position, ready to spring into action.

Then, just as suddenly as the strange lion had appeared, he quickly disappeared from view. One moment, he was there, and the next, he was gone. Rayah stayed hunkered down for a minute or two, then he slowly stood up. Charging to the edge of the wadi where the lion had been, he nosed around until he was satisfied that the intruder was indeed gone.

For the rest of the day, Rayah stayed close by Yeshua's side. Occasionally he would leap to the top of the ridge and look around in all directions, and then as though reassured that they were in no danger, he jumped back down again, only to take up a sentinel position alongside Yeshua.

The big lion's companionship was comforting to Yeshua as they sat side by side at the water's edge. He didn't feel like walking around much, so Yeshua spent the rest of the day dangling his feet in the cool water and singing psalms to Rayah. After Yeshua had recited the ninety-first psalm for at least the tenth time, Rayah finally relaxed and stretched out to rest.

The remainder of the evening was uneventful, but when darkness finally settled upon the wilderness, Yeshua curled up a little closer to the side of the wadi wall than usual to sleep. Tucked back under the overhang, somehow he felt a measure of security. Not that he was afraid, but the events of the day made him feel a little more wary than normal. He was thankful that Rayah showed no sign of leaving, but instead lay down in front of him like a living, breathing barricade.

Getting to sleep was harder than before. The darkness seemed to take on different ominous shapes, and every sound was amplified into a menacing threat. Yeshua lay staring into the night sky dimly lit by a thin, thumbnail-shaped moon. Inside, he was peaceful, but unrest swirled around in the shadows of the night keeping sleep at bay.

Well, if I can't get to sleep, I guess I will just quote the ninety-first psalm a few more times, Yeshua thought. Even though he loved every word of the Scriptures, this psalm was the one that never failed to bring peace and comfort.

"Addoni, I know I am in the secret place of Elyon and abide under the shadow of El Shaddai. I say of Jehovah, he is my refuge and my fortress: my Elohiym in him will I trust. I will not be afraid of the terror by night; nor of the arrow that flies by day; nor of the pestilence that walks in darkness; nor of the destruction or sudden death that surprises and lays waste at noonday. Because I have made Jehovah my refuge, even El Elyon my habitation, no evil shall befall me; for you give your angels charge over me to accompany, defend, and preserve me in all of my ways of obedience and service. They shall bear me up on their hands, lest I dash my foot against a stone. I shall tread upon the lion and adder; the young lion and the serpent I shall trample under feet. I will call upon you, and you will answer me and be with me in trouble. You will deliver me and honor me."

Before Yeshua had gotten completely through the psalm, he was sound asleep. He had not been asleep long, however, when he was jerked awake again by a bloodcurdling roar echoing throughout the valley. Immediately, Rayah snapped to attention with every muscle and sinew in his powerful body on alert. Lifting his massive head in the direction of the challenge, Rayah defiantly roared back his daring response.

Then all was quiet. Rayah stood motionless for some time listening and waiting. Yeshua finally decided that the prowling lion had left. Determined to get back to sleep, he lay back down. But sleep eluded him. Rayah was restless. He would drop down beside Yeshua for a few minutes then a little while later jump back up to pace back and forth along the wadi wall. This went on all night long with Yeshua drifting in and out of slumber until finally just before dawn, both Rayah and Yeshua fell sound asleep at last.

Periodically, over the next two days, the strange lion appeared on the crest of the ridge; sometimes, he would let loose his chilling roar, and at other times, he just stalked back and forth, threatening but biding his time. An air of foreboding gripped the wadi as Yeshua struggled to maintain his usual routine. He knew Rayah was probably getting hungry, but he shadowed Yeshua wherever he went, which wasn't very far considering the intruder who was lurking around.

By the third night, Yeshua had about convinced himself that the lion was no real threat and that he was just playing with their minds. In fact, he had decided that maybe it wasn't even real at all, but just a bizarre figment of their imagination, or worse yet, a malevolent spirit in the form of a lion. That seemed the more likely conclusion. After all, he was aware that his enemy, Satan, went about like a roaring lion seeking someone whom he might devour.

If that were the case, then there was certainly nothing to fear from him. By virtue of his right standing with Jehovah, he had unqualified authority over all the power of the enemy, and nothing could in any way harm him. Convinced that this was indeed the case, that night, he slept soundly for the first time in several nights. Even Rayah was not so restless.

Just as the sun began to send its golden rays over the edge of the wadi wall, Yeshua felt a chilling presence even before he opened his eyes. As he rolled over to look around, he saw standing on the edge of the water hole the very personification of evil watching them. The lion was almost twice the size of Rayah, unkempt with scraggly coarse hair covering his gigantic frame; his eyes were red like flaming coals of fire, and the air around about him smelled putrid with a sulfur-like odor.

Yeshua jumped to his feet, awakening Rayah in the process. Immediately sensing danger, Rayah leaped to his feet in a battle position. The hair down the ridge of his spine bristled as he roared a warning at the intruder.

Time stood still as they faced each other—one lion brave and courageous, the other defiant and arrogant. Yeshua recognized what was about to happen but felt powerless to stop it. By this time, he had gotten to know Rayah well enough to realize that his friend would never let anything encroach on his territory unchallenged.

With a shrill scream, Rayah sprang across the water hole, landing inches from the large lion. Within seconds, they were locked together in fierce combat. Round and round they went, snarling, biting, and clawing, each with fangs bared slicing at each other in a vicious life-and-death struggle.

Yeshua watched the valiant efforts of his companion and protector as if in slow motion. Time after time, Rayah came close to sinking his fangs into the jugular of the big cat, but each time, the intruder escaped and in the process sliced Rayah with his razor-sharp claws, ripping open the flesh along his side. After a short time of intense battle, Rayah started to weaken from loss of blood. In one unguarded moment, the big lion closed in on Rayah for the final blow. Seizing his neck, he secured a strangle hold on Rayah. Minutes later, it was all over. The heinous lion stood over Rayah's body in proud defiance, flinging his head as he let out a roar of triumph.

Then he turned to face Yeshua. His evil, mocking countenance seemed to take on superhuman intelligence as his flaming eyes glared at Yeshua in a sneer of elation. Not intimidated,

Yeshua didn't move a muscle but boldly fixed his eyes on his adversary. Then in holy, righteous anger, he fearlessly addressed the wicked creature standing before him. "You master of deception and wickedness, you enemy of everything that is good—be gone from my sight!"

Then almost as though the lion had been struck in the face with a sword, he gave a yelp of surprise then raced away as though in terror, disappearing over the ridge.

Yeshua knelt by the still body of his friend and companion. Lifting his eyes to heaven, he cried out, "Elohiym, why didn't you protect him from the evil one? Rayah was my friend. He gave his life trying to protect me. Why did this happen?"

Even as Yeshua lifted his cry of anguish heavenward, down inside he already knew the answer. Evil and death had been loosed in the world centuries ago, and until that cycle was broken, heartache and sorrow would always be the result. In that moment of grief, Yeshua was touched with the feeling of the infirmities of mankind. There in his wilderness sanctuary, he had experienced the intrusion of death. In the depths of his emotions, he became aware of the pain and agony that comes from the wicked reign of the ruler of darkness.

As he buried his face in Rayah's mane, he resolved once again to do whatever it took to snatch the keys of death from the usurper and place authority once again in the hands of redeemed mankind—the ones who Jehovah had granted the right to be the legal rulers over the earth in the beginning.

Chapter Eleven

The nearest Yeshua could calculate, it had been about forty days since he had entered that barren wilderness. Even though his spirit remained strong, his body had begun to weaken with no food to sustain it. After the tragic encounter with the renegade lion, Yeshua had considered raising Rayah from the dead. He knew his heavenly Father was the giver of life, but the Holy Spirit did not direct him to perform that miracle. Instead, he had dragged the lifeless body of his courageous friend and defender along the wadi floor until he had come to a small indention hollowed out at the foot of the wall. There, he had respectfully laid Rayah to rest at the back of the cave. Then erecting a formation of rocks over the entrance, he sealed off the burial place from any prowling scavengers.

With a heavy heart, Yeshua trudged sorrowfully back to the location where he and Rayah had spent many pleasant hours. As he approached the water hole where they had splashed together only days before, it now appeared to have shrunken in size, and the whole area seemed empty and bleak.

Yeshua threw himself down on the hard ground under the ledge and tried to pray, but the words would not come. It had been so long since he had heard the voice of his heavenly Father that he was beginning to have some doubts about who he really was or why he had even come here in the first place.

Had a dove really descended from heaven only weeks before, and had he in fact heard a heavenly voice? Or was the incident with the dove only a coincidence; had he just imagined the voice? Some had thought it had just thundered. Maybe nothing that he thought had happened was what had really taken place.

Thoughts of doubt swirled through his head like waves crashing against the shoreline, threatening to crush his resolve and destroy his faith. As if sensing the agitation going on inside his mind, overhead, the winds began to stir. The sun that had just emerged over the east end of the wadi wall appeared to be a deep orange, casting an unnatural glare over the valley walls.

Glancing at the distant sky, Yeshua could see that a dreaded *khamsin*, or as the Hebrews call it a *sharav*, was blowing in from the southeast. This time of year when those fierce, scorching winds howled for hours at a time, the suffocating walls of dust and grains of sand could become both suffocating and blinding.

Having lived through many such events, Yeshua took off his girdle and dipped it in the pool of water. Wrapping it around his nose and mouth, he scooted as far back under the ledge as he could and prepared to wait out the tempest.

There, curled in a tight knot with his face between his knees, he could hear the roar of the gale above the wadi as it gained speed and strength. Strong gusts of wind scraped the wadi floor, causing debris and powdery dirt to become airborne as it swirled throughout the valley creating a churning, twisting funnel of dust.

When Yeshua had encountered the first *khamsin* at the beginning of his time in the wilderness, he had simply curled up in a peaceful sleep until it had blown itself out. But this time, he felt no peace. In the midst of the howling winds, troubling thoughts continued to bombard his mind as small grains of sand incessantly stung his exposed flesh.

The tormenting thoughts that assailed his mind were completely foreign to his normal thought patterns. Never once in all of the years since he had had that first visitation from his heavenly Father had he ever doubted the reality of what he had been told. Why now was his mind questioning what he knew to be the truth?

As the wind screamed around his head, it seemed that Yeshua could hear in the midst of the tempest the clamor of taunting voices—railing, questioning, and confusing voices trying to stir up inside his mind a storm of negativity that equaled the furor of the *khamsin*. Yeshua could feel the suffocating presence of unseen beings pressing in from every side—creatures full of evil resolve, malevolent by nature, intent on tormenting him as he sat in desolation, huddled against the wadi wall.

Yeshua clamped his hands over his ears, but the voices persisted. "You are a pitiful piece of humanity. How can anything you could possibly do change the human race, let alone even one person? You don't even have a plan. You are a nobody; a commoner; born in a stable. No one will want to hear what you have to say. How can you ever convince anyone that you are the Son of God, if indeed you really are God's Son?"

The voices rose and fell, tearing at his mind while the shrieking gale-force winds yanked violently at Yeshua's garments. The oppression closed in on Yeshua like a predator circling ever closer and closer, anticipating the final attack for the kill.

But as brutal as the assault was, and as persuasive as the voices were, Yeshua was not about to crack. As surely as he could recognize the voice of his heavenly Father, he could also identify the schemes of his adversary. All those whispers of skepticism, misgiving, and uncertainty were not coming from inside; they were poisonous propaganda covertly endeavoring to infect his thought life. More importantly, he knew what to do to stop it.

With renewed boldness and deliberate determination, Yeshua raised his head and confronted the vortex of darkness that looked as if malicious creatures were pushing against the thin veil that separated the spirit realm from the physical.

In a commanding voice, Yeshua cried out into the wind, "I know where I came from, and where I am going. I do not judge according to the flesh or by earthly standards. The testimony I bear of myself, I am not alone in making it. There are two of us: I and the Father who sent me."

Even though Yeshua's words were flung back in his face by the force of the gale, he continued, "I did not even come on my own authority or of my own accord, but it is the heavenly Father who sent me. You tempters are from the devil, and he does not stand in the truth because there is no truth in him. He is a liar and the father of lies and of all that is false."

Yeshua felt wonderful life-giving strength and confidence begin to pour into every part of his being as the truth began to do its work of freedom in his mind. He could sense the anointing of the Holy Spirit stirring once again. He jumped to his feet not even noticing that the cloth had dropped from around his face. Standing with arms lifted to heaven against the driving winds of the *khamsin*, he shouted, "In you, O Jehovah, do I put my trust and confidently take refuge; let me never be put to shame or confusion! My soul takes refuge and finds shelter and confidence in you; yes, in the shadow of your wings will I take refuge and be confident until calamities and destructive storms are passed."

With that pronouncement, a holy boldness came over him. Even though he couldn't see the tormenting spirits, he could still discern their hovering presence. Addressing them with the authority that came from heaven, he commanded, "Get behind me, you messengers of Satan. You are not on Jehovah's side, but instead you have come to promote the schemes of darkness. Be gone!"

Instantly, the heavy oppression that had filled Yeshua's wadi sanctuary was gone. In its place was a sense of lightness and freedom. Yeshua could tell that his accusers had fled. There was no darkness anywhere. The thrill of victory overwhelmed Yeshua, causing him to rejoice there in the midst of the storm. "I have cried unto you, Elohiym Elyon, who performs on my behalf and rewards me; who brings to pass your purposes for me and surely completes them."

Then with the Holy Spirit stirring and empowering him from within, he addressed the raging wind that had become the instrument of evil. With a loud voice, he commanded, "Peace, be still."

Just as suddenly as the *khamsin* had begun, just that quickly the wind ceased, and there was a great calm. The sun shone unobstructed overhead again, and the peace surrounding him was firmly established inside his heart once more.

Yeshua couldn't keep his feet still. Running back and forth along the wadi floor, he sang at the top of his lungs, "Jehovah has given unyielding and impenetrable strength to his people; Jehovah has blessed me with peace."

Then whirling around in pure delight, he lifted his hands and voice heavenward and sang, "Jehovah, you have redeemed my life in peace from the battle that was against me so that none came near me, for they were many who strove with me. You have turned my mourning into dancing. You have girded me with gladness to the end that my tongue and my heart and everything glorious within me may sing praises unto you and not be silent. O Jehovah, my Elohiym, I will give thanks to you forever."

The longer he sang, the stronger he felt. In fact, he could identify with the psalmist David, who wrote, "I can run through a troop, and with Jehovah, I can leap over a wall!"

For the rest of the day, Yeshua could not keep still. He walked and sang. He even climbed to the top of the wadi wall and preached to the barren hills proclaiming the power of the kingdom of God and the impending defeat coming to the kingdom of darkness. If it had not been for the restraining power of the Holy Spirit inside, Yeshua would have grabbed his staff and ran out of that wilderness to find someone he could bless.

But he knew his time was not yet. Yeshua was fully committed to do only what the Father told him to do and say only what the father instructed. In his heart, he knew that something more needed to take place before he would be released into ministry; he didn't know what. However, he knew it was something of great importance, and that it would probably be extremely challenging. But he didn't care. He was thoroughly convinced that greater was the one that was within him than any wickedness that was in the world. He had proved it today, and he was ready.

Chapter Twelve

The next morning, Yeshua was surprised to awake with hunger pangs gnawing at his belly. During the past forty days, he had hardly thought about food. In fact, his focus had been primarily on spiritual things, so he had paid very little attention to any discomfort in his body. But that morning, it was as though his body was screaming at him with a newly discovered voice.

As the morning wore on, hunger became a ravenous beast, demanding and insistent, refusing to be ignored. Yeshua walked up and down the wadi floor looking for anything that might be edible. He was aware that after a prolonged fast, when hunger returns, the body is on the verge of starvation. Yeshua was sure that Jehovah had not sent him out into this forsaken desert to starve.

Everywhere Yeshua looked, he was unable to uncover even so much as a berry bush. Nothing—there was no food to be had. The area had been named correctly; it was in every way a wilderness. Returning to the water hole, Yeshua tried filling his empty stomach with water, but it rebelled. He needed nourishment. Drained of energy, he collapsed on a flat rock positioned at the water's edge.

His hunger reminded him of the plight of the children of Israel when they were in the wilderness. They had had no food either, and Jehovah had provided manna for them.

Well, it's time for a little manna here in this wilderness, he thought wistfully.

As he sat there thinking about manna, his attention was drawn to a pile of smooth, round rocks situated close to the water's edge. Was his imagination playing tricks on him, or did they actually resemble the barley loaves his mother used to make?

She had been celebrated as one of the best bread makers in the whole town of Nazareth. The tantalizing aroma of her fresh-baked bread could tempt a person even before he entered the house. Without ever taking a bite, you could almost taste the mouthwatering morsel of hearty bread slathered with goat's butter, hot and dripping with honey.

Yeshua's senses had recreated the memory of the barley loaves with such detail that his mouth started to water. He had been so caught up in the culinary vision that he didn't even realized that he had picked up one of the round stones. He was staring at it, wondering how it had gotten there, when all at once, a cloud covered the sun. Shadowy images danced against the wadi walls, and a pall blanketed the atmosphere.

Yeshua looked up at the sun overhead; it was still shining, but something was happening; he could feel it.

What Yeshua could not see with his eyes but could clearly discern in his spirit were hordes of invisible beings that had gathered from all regions of the second and third heavens and even from the ends of the earth. Evil, wicked spirits along with hosts of holy angels from heaven had come to witness the battle of the ages. The outcome would determine the destiny of mankind for eternities to come.

Unaware of events that were to come or of the spectators gathered to observe, Yeshua arose from where he had been seated by the pond of water. As he set out to investigate the strange phenomenon he had felt in the atmosphere, suddenly, he froze. Directly in front of him a dazzlingly beautiful creature materialized before his eyes.

Startled, Yeshua found himself staring at an individual with hair that looked like fine-spun gold, whose countenance was alluring by any standard. From head to toe, the being was clothed with an exquisite crimson robe girded about with a belt of gold, but the eyes were sinister like coals of fire. They resembled the eyes of a snake—wicked but fascinating at the same time. His proud body was straight, and his hands were smooth like a woman's hands. Shimmering sandals of gold graced his feet. Even though he was a beautiful creature indeed, Yeshua could tell right away that he was evil personified. Then he knew that standing in front of him was Satan himself.

"So we meet again." Satan addressed Yeshua in a honey-coated tone that was both cunning and seductive.

Yes, Yeshua remembered where he had seen that countenance before. In his visit to heaven, he had watched that same creature, who was the most celebrated archangel in heaven, change into the supreme renegade of the universe. He had seen Lucifer fall like lightning and become the notorious usurper on planet earth. In the ages past, before Yeshua had been born a man, he was aware that he had known Lucifer quite well. They most certainly had met before.

Then in a smooth velvety voice, Satan interrupted Yeshua's thoughts. Pointing to the stone that Yeshua still held in his hand, he suggested, "It looks like a delicious loaf of bread, does it not?" His motions were suggestive as he took a step closer to where Yeshua stood.

Instinctively, Yeshua moved backward and in the process almost tripped over a large, jagged rock that was in his way. He caught himself just in time to keep from falling but realized what an awkward picture he had made.

Satan snickered disdainfully and then asked in a mocking tone, "So you think you are the Son of God, do you?"

When Yeshua did not answer, he continued. "If you really are God's Son, why don't you command these stones to be made into loaves of bread?" He motioned to the pile of rounded rocks by the water's edge.

Looking from the pile of rocks to the stone still clutched in his hand, Yeshua could almost taste the loaf of bread. He was convinced that should he give the command, it was likely that a miracle would take place, and his ravenous hunger would be more than satisfied. He could literally feel the strong pull his growling stomach was making on his will. Reason added its voice, arguing that nothing could possibly be wrong with a simple little miracle to satisfy a legitimate need.

But then, that was the way Adam and Eve had rationalized too. They were supposed to have gotten their directions from God, but in order to satisfy their flesh, they had decided what they were going to do on their own—completely apart from God's command. Choosing to make decisions without God had gotten the world in the mess it was in now.

Besides, Satan was challenging him to prove who he was by performing a miracle. Yeshua had already settled that matter firmly in his mind yesterday, and he certainly didn't need to convince Satan that he was the Son of God. Lucifer, turned Satan, would know that for a fact soon enough.

Because Yeshua had resolved many years back to do only what his heavenly Father wanted done and say only what the Father instructed him to say, he cast the stone that was in his hand as far away as he could throw it. Then with steadfast determination, he replied, "It is written, 'Man shall not live and be sustained by bread alone but by every word that comes forth from the mouth of God.'"

At Yeshua's strong declaration of the Word of God, Satan almost lost his composure. This time, it was he who stumbled backward as though he had been struck with a tangible weapon. For just an instant, Yeshua could tell that Satan was infuriated, but then he regained his poise and approached Yeshua for the second time.

Without any prior warning, Yeshua found that he had been transported in an instant to the tallest point of the temple in Jerusalem. He could tell where he was because standing there on the pinnacle he could see they were overlooking a scene he was familiar with. On his right, he viewed the Court of the Gentiles, which was teeming with vendors selling souvenirs, sacrificial animals, and food, as well as currency changers who were exchanging

Roman coins for Jewish money. Here and there guides were providing tours of the premises. He easily identified the ever-present priests, or *kohanim*, in their white linen robes and tubular hats scurrying here and there, directing and advising pilgrims about the different kinds of sacrifices to be performed, completely unaware of what was going on overhead.

Yeshua could also clearly see a crowd of Jewish women and men dancing and singing to lively music in the Court of the Women. On the south side of the Temple Mount complex, he viewed a steady stream of pilgrims going in and out of the public entrance.

"You see what a busy place this is," Satan pointed out in a charming voice. "This would be a wonderful place to start your ministry. Why, a spectacular demonstration of your marvelous power would get the attention of the world."

Then Satan fixed his eyes on Yeshua with a hypnotic stare. In his most persuasive manner, he offered, "If you are who you say you are…if you are the Son of God, throw yourself down, for it is written, 'He will give his angels charge over you, and they will bear you up on their hands lest you strike your foot against a stone.'"

Yeshua was astonished to hear scripture coming out of the mouth of the adversary of truth. Yeshua believed every word of the sacred writings of the psalmist, but somehow, it sounded different when filtered through the voice of the evil one.

As he stood looking down at the religious activity of the very ones he had come to save, he recalled the words of his heavenly Father: "You will be rejected and forsaken by men. The very ones you have come to save will scorn you and will not appreciate your worth. You will be afflicted, and the judgment of mankind will fall upon you. You will be wounded for transgressions and bruised for iniquities, scourged so that people can be healed and made whole. Then finally, you will be betrayed and cruelly crucified on a cross with the consent of the religious leaders, ridiculed by your people, and tormented by ruthless Roman soldiers."

There was certainly nothing appealing about what lay ahead for his ministry if he did it Jehovah's way. Yeshua hadn't intended on giving any thought to the suggestions of Satan, but there was something about his presence that had a strange, persuasive effect. Reason entered the conversation. *If you jump from this pinnacle in full view of the Sanhedrin and all of the religious leaders, they would without doubt applaud you as the Messiah when you land unhurt.*

It really was an appealing plan. What an easy way to convince them that he was the Son of God. After all, it is not necessarily the way one does a thing that is important; it is the end result that counts.

Yeshua moved closer to the edge of the pinnacle. Looking down some two hundred feet, he could see tiny figures of humanity who had gathered from distant lands scurrying to and fro, unaware that their savior was poised directly above. Yeshua loved them. He desperately wanted them to accept him, but accept him for what? As the great superman, the Messiah, or the sacrificial lamb that would take away their sins?

Of course! The trap was finally clear to Yeshua. A super-Messiah would be no good to mankind unless they could be redeemed from sin. Yeshua could play the part of Messiah in a breathtaking, spectacular way, but humanity would remain helpless under the rule of the prince of darkness without hope and without God in the world.

Yeshua whirled around and faced Satan. With eyes flashing, he shouted from the depths of his spirit that was synchronized with the compassionate beat of his heavenly Father's heart, "It is indeed written that angels will bear me up on their hands lest I strike my foot against a stone. On the other hand, it is also written, 'You shall not tempt the Lord your God.'"

The gleeful expression on Satan's face, who was obviously anticipating victory, quickly changed to painful surprise. As the eternal word sliced through the air, Satan doubled over in agony. The next thing Yeshua knew, he was standing beside the pool of water in the wilderness wadi, once again, alone.

But Yeshua knew he was not alone. He could feel the ministry of unseen angels strengthening him and preparing him for what was to come next. He knew the nature of his chief adversary was not to give up so easily. Satan would be back. In the meantime, Yeshua was content to bask in the smile of his heavenly Father.

Chapter Thirteen

Hunger became a furious cannibal tearing at Yeshua's organs, directing his quest for food to a level of intensity that refused to allow his mind to think on anything else. His encounter with Satan had weakened him even though he had triumphed. He knew it was important to build his spirit up again through prayer and meditating on the Word, but the discomfort in his body was screaming so loud that his mind was having trouble concentrating.

He trudged up and down the wadi floor looking in every crevice for something to fill the hollowness in his belly. Even a locust or a grasshopper would do—but he found nothing. It was as though he had been transported to a place where there was nothing alive. The vegetation that had sparsely graced the nooks of the wadi wall weeks before had even been whipped to nothingness by the recent *khamsin*.

Exhausted by his efforts, Yeshua finally dragged himself back to the waterhole that was day by day evaporating in the wilderness heat. He collapsed by its edge, feeling too weak to even get up again. Hours passed. Still, Yeshua did not move. He found that it was a struggle to even pray—yet he knew he must.

I can't just lie here and die, he thought.

With as much effort as he could muster, he whispered, "My Father, I need help. Please…strengthen my mortal body."

Faith without works is dead, that much he knew. So he rolled over on his stomach and pushed his emaciated body onto his hands and knees. Then inch by inch, he crawled to the large rock situated close by and eased himself to a sitting position.

With head hanging, he sat there panting, waiting for Jehovah to answer his prayer. Yeshua had never experienced before the forceful influence a person's body could have on his mind and spirit. In his thirty years of life, he had had to endure only very little physical pain—and he had never been this hungry.

I have waited too long to get out of this dessert alive, he thought. *Now I can't even climb up to the top of the wadi. I could die here, and no one except my heavenly Father would ever know.*

Over and over he had to remind himself that Jehovah had a purpose for him even here in this wilderness—but that purpose was becoming less appealing by the hour. At the moment, becoming the savior of the world seemed like a far-fetched, idealist delusion.

He had sat there for only a few minutes when he felt the atmosphere change. The heat that had been stifling before now crushed in from all sides, squeezing from him what was left of his strength.

The longer he sat, the more lightheaded he felt. He finally decided to lie back down by the waterhole. Pushing himself to a standing position, he managed to take one faltering step when he was startled by someone addressing him from behind.

"Having a nice day?" the voice asked.

Yeshua almost fell as he carefully turned to see the source of the inquiry. There in all his resplendent arrogance stood Satan once again. He was as beautiful as he had been on the first encounter, and if anything, looking even more powerful than before. His very presence exuded a seducing quality that was magnetic.

"How do you feel today?" Satan asked in a soft, smooth voice.

Then with a pained expression pasted on his face, he said, "You don't look so good. I know you have been asking Jehovah to help you, but you will notice he has not lifted a finger to do anything for you."

Satan took a step closer to Yeshua. Holding out his hands in an enticing manner, he said in a beguiling tone, "But I am here. And I can help you."

Satan made his way to Yeshua's side. When he touched Yeshua's arm as though to steady him, they were transported to the top of a high mountain in the twinkling of an eye. Yeshua did not recognize the location, but he could tell they were somewhere at a height that towered far above the surrounding landscape. He knew he had not left his body behind because he still felt dizzy, as weak as ever, and just as hungry.

In his weakened condition, the thought that he was in the presence of his enemy wasn't registering as vividly as it had before. Actually, Satan didn't even seem as evil as Yeshua had remembered. In fact, Yeshua was having a struggle remembering anything at all. Besides, at that moment, Satan appeared to be more of an angel of light than an emissary of darkness.

"Let's talk for a while about your mission," Satan said in a friendly manner. "I know you are here because you want to save the world. And I suppose it does need saving."

Yeshua's senses felt lifeless, and the voice he was hearing seemed dreamlike. Stumbling to a rocky rise on the mountain, he dropped down beside a small bush and buried his face in his hands.

Satan knelt down on one knee to address him eye to eye. "I know it was a sad day for God when he watched the kingdoms of this world slip from his hands. That is why you are here, is it not? To win them back for him?"

Yeshua lifted his head for a moment but couldn't recall anything about Jehovah wanting the world's kingdoms. "I'm…I'm not sure what you are talking about," he mumbled.

"Okay, let me put it this way. God wants authority over the entire planet once again, but I have it. He sent you to get it. It's that simple."

Yeshua gave his head a shake to try to clear his mind. Is that really why he was here, to govern the kingdoms of the world? Dominion was the issue—but what kind of dominion?

As if Satan could read his thoughts, he pulled Yeshua to his feet and led him to a spot where he could see a panoramic view of what lay beyond the mountain. In a moment of time, the

glory, the splendor, and the magnificence of each of the kingdoms of the world paraded before his sight. He saw glittering
horse-drawn chariots, splendid palaces, and massive armies of
the Roman and Greek empires. There were coffers filled with
wealth from Assyria and the marvels of Egypt and beyond. One
by one, they all passed before his vision.

"See all of this glory," Satan said with great flourish. "This
is what you came to get. Just how do you propose to accomplish that?"

Even though Yeshua was fighting confusion, a picture came
into his mind that was forever etched there. He recalled the
image of Symeon the Rabbi nailed to the side of his house with
arms and feet impaled with cruel spikes. He could still hear the
tormenting screams that came from his bloody lips as his body
writhed, racked with pain, and that was what he had to look
forward to.

Yeshua remembered the anguish of his heavenly Father when
he had told him of the betrayal, shame, and ridicule that lay ahead
for him; the pain on the Father's face while warning him of the
torture and crucifixion that was inevitable.

He had offered his body as a sacrifice then and glibly submit-
ted to a plan that included incredible suffering. But now, his body
was distressed because of the first stages of starvation, and that
was only a minuscule amount of suffering compared to what he
would have to endure in the end.

Satan interrupted Yeshua's flow of thought, and in a tone
brimming with intrigue, said, "If you want all of this power and
authority, I will give it to you—for as you know, it has been turned
over to me, and I am at liberty to give it to whoever I will."

"You…you are offering me all of the kingdoms of the world
just like that?" Yeshua asked weakly, endeavoring to concentrate
and process what he was hearing.

Forcing himself to remain in a standing position, Yeshua once
again considered the images parading their grandeur as far as his

eye could see. How could the Father's plan for redeeming the world, consisting of torment and a savage death, be better than what he was being presented with now?

"You can slaughter all the lambs in the world and offer them up to your God, and he could never give you all of this. Do obeisance to me only once, and I will make you ruler over everything."

Yeshua turned from the spectacular view and focused on the being that stood before him. Satan's very presence exuded power. With his pomp and arrogance, he exhibited a commanding demeanor that flaunted authority. Satan's hypnotic aura in addition to Yeshua's weakened state was eating away at his resolve.

Fall down before him one time and gain the whole world, Yeshua thought. *What harm could that do? One time and one time only would give the Father what he wanted without the pain.*

> The spirit beings that had gathered from the reaches of the second and third heavens pressed in closer to the veil that separated the physical from the spirit realm. Hosts of angels and a contingent of the hordes of hell that had been following the events of this epic struggle between the two kingdoms—the domain of darkness and the sphere of light—now gasped as they realized what was at stake in the next few minutes. What was about to happen would determine the destiny of mankind forever and the fate of the whole universe. It was in the hands of one man. His choice would seal the fate of the world. And no one was allowed to interfere from the spirit realm—not angels, or demons, not even Jehovah himself. The decision rested in the hands of Yeshua; he, and he alone, was the only one who could change the world.

Minutes passed in complete silence. Satan had never been known to be patient. But now he must have realized that his plan was at a critical point, perhaps aware that Yeshua was weakening because he remained motionless.

Once again, Yeshua studied the scenes before him. Something gnawed at the edge of his consciousness. As appealing as what he was looking at seemed, something was stirring inside his heart. So he waited.

Then from the recesses of his spirit, words that had been hidden there over the years exploded into his mind: *What does it profit a man to gain the whole world and then lose his own soul?*

Soul! Of course, that's what this is all about—not just my soul, but the souls of mankind. None of this is about kingdoms—about wealth and glory. Dominion is not just ruling over people. It's about ruling over evil and Satan's kingdom.

Strength from the living Word began to flow into Yeshua's inner man. The influence of its reality in his heart spread enlightenment to his mind.

If I fall down before Satan even once, yes, he might hand me everything, but then I, and all that he could give me, would still be under his control. The whole world would perish and heaven along with it. And what about sin? Sin would still govern the earth without a solution.

Yeshua jerked his attention from the gaudy display of worldly goods to stare intently at the confident figure standing before him. Satan was the epitome of haughtiness. Decked out in ridiculous pageantry, he was already showing signs of impending victory by the smirk registering on his countenance.

How could I have even considered for one instant taking the easy way out? Yeshua thought as he surveyed the master deceiver.

The veil had fallen from his eyes; now Yeshua could clearly see the truth—there was no easy way. Only the death of an innocent lamb could redeem mankind. He had come not to rule mankind but to become that lamb—the Lamb of God to take away the sins of the world. It was completely clear now. If he bowed down to Satan, he would no longer be innocent; but like Adam and Eve, he would be tainted and no longer eligible to become the heaven-sent sacrificial lamb.

Righteous indignation arose within Yeshua that both angered and invigorated him. His eyes flashed with holy fire, and the fierceness of his countenance caused Satan to tremble.

Then out of Yeshua's mouth came the Word of God, like a sharp, two-edged sword ripping through the heavens, sealing the victory for the kingdom of God. "Get behind me, Satan!" he said. "It is written, 'You shall worship the Lord your God; and *him only* shall you serve.'"

The force of light that shot from Yeshua's mouth hit Satan with such power that he was propelled backward so that he could not remain upright. Instead of Yeshua bowing before him, Satan found himself prostrate at Yeshua's feet.

Humiliated and disgraced, Satan quickly disappeared into the second heaven to regroup and once again come up with a new strategy: waiting for another, more opportune and favorable time.

Chapter Fourteen

The next thing Yeshua knew, he was back in the wilderness once again surrounded by the scenery he had grown so familiar with over the past month and a half.

The thrill of victory he had achieved over the seducer made him appreciate his earthly parents and the rabbis who had faithfully instilled the Torah in his young heart. Thankful that they had insisted he memorize those words that were so alive and full of power—words capable of becoming a sharp, penetrating weapon when spoken from the mouth of one who believes.

Yeshua glanced around at his wilderness hideaway, and although it looked the same, something was different. The atmosphere that had been hot and stifling now felt charged with vibrant life as though the last remains of dark forces had been dispelled.

Though Yeshua's inner man had been revitalized spiritually, his outer man was still ravenous. However, the frantic need to satisfy that hunger didn't seem to matter so much anymore.

Yeshua knelt beside a rock. Even though his body was weakened from hunger, still, he lifted his hands the best he could in praise to his heavenly Father. "Now I know, O Jehovah, that you save your anointed; you have answered me from your holy heaven with the saving strength of your right hand."

Tears of thanksgiving trickled down Yeshua's face as psalms of praise poured unhindered from deep inside. "My Father, your way is perfect. Your Word is tested and tried; you are a shield to all those who take refuge and put their trust in you."

Then completely overcome with adoration for his heavenly Father, he continued, "I love you fervently and devotedly, O Jehovah, my strength. You are my rock, my fortress, and my deliverer; my Elohiym, in whom I will trust and take refuge, my shield, and the horn of my salvation, my high tower."

The more Yeshua praised, the stronger he felt. He jumped to his feet with his face lifted heavenward and fairly shouted, "You have drawn me up out of a horrible pit and set my feet upon a rock, steadying my steps and establishing my goings. You have put a new song in my mouth, a song of praise to you, my Father."

Joy bubbled out of Yeshua's spirit wiping away the last traces of fatigue. "I delight to do your will, O my Elohiym; yes, your law is within my heart."

With hands still lifted toward heaven, Yeshua sensed something or someone standing at his side. When he opened his eyes, he beheld an angel of Jehovah standing before him. The being was well over seven feet tall, dressed in a shimmering white tunic with a luminous golden belt around his waist. Beneath white trousers shone bronze shoes. His hair appeared to be flaxen, and his skin was the color of burnished brass glowing from the radiance that came from being in the presence of Jehovah himself.

Yeshua looked into eyes that were like balls of fire, but at the same time, they were filled with such warm compassion that he could literally feel the angel's gaze.

The angel knelt before Yeshua, addressing him in a tone of great reverence. "Most Holy One, I have been sent from the great Jehovah in answer to your prayer for strength."

So he did hear my feeble prayer after all, Yeshua thought. Again, he was thankful he had not believed the insinuations of Satan that had suggested his heavenly Father was not going to be faithful.

"Jehovah has sent me to strengthen you." The angel stood and held out to Yeshua a round wafer that looked very much like some type of bread.

"Eat all of it," instructed the angel. "It will give you energy for the journey ahead."

Yeshua eagerly ate the wafer, savoring the first bite of food that had crossed his lips for over forty days. He found that it was delicious like fresh-baked bread made with the finest honey. When Yeshua finished the portion of food, the angel then handed him a silver ladle filled with what appeared to be water.

When Yeshua finished drinking every drop of it, he felt a sensation race throughout his body that was both invigorating and exhilarating. Its immediate effect was to intensify the joy and thanksgiving that Yeshua already had been experiencing. Once again, he couldn't keep from lifting his hands to praise and worship Jehovah with uninhibited enthusiasm.

I must have just had a drink from the river of life that comes from the throne of Jehovah, Yeshua thought. He could feel the Holy Spirit flowing from his innermost being like streams of living water.

He didn't even know when the angel left. He was so caught up in glorifying his heavenly Father that he was not aware of anything except his overpowering affection and adoration for the one who loved him so completely. He didn't know how long he stood magnifying Jehovah with arms reaching to heaven, but he was aware that his hunger was gone, and he felt stronger than he ever had before.

As Yeshua continued his exaltation heavenward, he noticed a luminous cloud descending upon the wadi that continued to widen until it permeated every inch of it. A delightful fragrance like that of the Rose of Sharon spread throughout the area. Then out of the midst of the cloud, for the first time since he had entered the wasteland, Yeshua heard the voice of his beloved Father.

Jehovah's voice thundered throughout the cavernous areas of the wadi, filling the surroundings with his presence. "Well done, my Son, I am highly pleased with you."

Jehovah's voice sounded like a symphony to Yeshua's ears—as melodious as a thousand harps raised in a glorious musical composition.

Jehovah continued. "Satan has tried to sift you like wheat, but you have passed the test. Your faith did not fail, and you remained obedient to my Word."

"Thank you, Father," Yeshua exhaled in relief. "It is good to hear you speak again. I know you had a good reason for your silence, but why did you not answer me before?"

"I was never far from you, my Son, but it was important that you face your toughest challenge as a man, not as God. It was vital that you walk by faith alone and not by sight. With my Word hidden in your heart, you have found that *it* is quite capable of keeping you during your hours of great temptation. You have been tested in every respect, yet you did not sin."

Yeshua gave a slight nod of his head. "You are right, of course. Your written Word is every bit as powerful as your voice; it is filled with your power, too."

Then as though scales had fallen from Yeshua's eyes, in a flash, he understood why he had been led to this wilderness. Now he could fully sympathize with each of mankind's infirmities and genuinely identify with their susceptibility to the assaults of temptation. He had endured the full cycle of temptation. He could still hear his old rabbi patiently recounting them over and over to the class one by one.

"The *lust of the flesh*," he said, "is the craving for sensual gratification, and the *lust of the eyes* is the greedy longings of the mind, whereas the *pride of life* is assurance in one's own resources or in the stability of earthly things that are in the world. These my children are what you will face in life; the things you must overcome."

Yeshua had borne the full blunt of Satan's arsenal, and he had triumphed.

"Now, because you have suffered being tempted," the heavenly Father said, "you will be able to immediately run to the cry for assistance from those who are being tempted. You, my Son, will be a merciful and faithful high priest for broken humanity."

By now, Yeshua was practically jumping inside with relief, not only from hearing his Father's voice again, but also from the love that poured over Yeshua's battered soul, comforting him like a mother cuddling the child she adores.

The warmth of the cloud enveloping Yeshua increased until it felt like a hand resting upon his head in benediction. He fell to his knees under its influence. Then a sensation like warm oil poured over his head, coursing down the full length of his body. In that state of submission and elation came the blessing and the commission of the heavenly Father.

"I am sending you forth anointed with the Holy Ghost and with power. You are to go from this place and heal all that are oppressed by the devil. Preach the good news to the poor, bind up and mend their broken hearts, and set at liberty the ones that are bruised."

The words that were spoken seemed like beams of light that penetrated Yeshua's whole being.

"You are to proclaim release to the physical and spiritual captives and recovery of sight to the blind and send forth delivered those who are oppressed, bruised, and broken down by calamity. Freely you have received; now freely give."

With that final pronouncement, the cloud lifted until Yeshua realized that once again, he was alone. But he knew he was not really alone. He was clothed from on high with the Holy Spirit, empowered to finally leave this desert and enter into the ministry he had come to the earth to fulfill.

He stayed on his knees for a few more minutes, letting the whole impact of what he had just experienced sink in. But what was stirring inside would not allow him to remain idle for long. With his walking stick in his hand, he walked out of the wilderness taking the same path that had led him in. However, the man that walked out was not the same one that walked in.

Yeshua had entered the wilderness as a man filled with the Holy Spirit, but left, the Messiah of mankind, tested to the core of his being, ready to reveal the character and will of his heavenly Father to the world.

As he went up out of the wilderness into Galilee full of the Holy Spirit, his fame spread throughout the whole region round about. The people who sat enveloped in darkness saw a great light, and for those who sat in the land of death, light had dawned.

Chapter Fifteen

Not everyone was happy to see that light. In fact, the illumination that emanated from Yeshua was downright maddening to the rulers of the darkness of the world. Its brilliance was disturbing the well-ordered structure of wickedness in Satan's kingdom, causing upheaval everywhere it went.

After Satan's disastrous encounter with the supposed Son of God on the mountaintop, he had to rethink this Messiah thing. How could a man made of flesh and blood resist his most sophisticated enticements? Flesh was theoretically weak. That was mankind's greatest stumbling block. A human's main instrument for sin was his flesh—at least, the lusts thereof. But Yeshua hadn't yielded, even when he had been at his weakest. How could that be?

Maybe an indirect approach would work better, Satan thought. So he gathered his strongest demons and sent them out to follow Yeshua around. There had to be a weak point somewhere.

They couldn't even get close to him. Everywhere he went, strong, warring angels surrounded him. In fact, the first place Yeshua traveled to after leaving the wilderness was his hometown. He immediately entered the synagogue in Nazareth and preached. It hadn't been too hard to stir up the religious hypocrites there. They grew so enraged when Yeshua proclaimed himself to be the anointed one that they tried to hurl him headlong over the cliff. But angels formed a barrier around him while he passed right through the midst of the agitated crowd without a scratch and went on his way.

Next, Yeshua went to the synagogue in Capernaum where Satan had one of his captives stationed: a man that had played around in sin so long that some especially foul spirits had been able to take possession of him. When Yeshua entered the building, the demons couldn't keep quiet, and that was their undoing.

They cried out with a loud cry, "Ah, let us alone! What have you to do with us, Yeshua of Nazareth? Have you come to destroy us? We know who you are—the Holy One of God."

What possessed them to say that? Satan didn't know. Right away, they found out what Satan had been suspecting: Yeshua had the same authority and power that Jehovah had given to Adam and Eve in the beginning. As soon as Yeshua rebuked the demons, they lost their hold over the man. They had no choice but to leave.

Hoards of demons clamored in Satan's ears. "Where was all this power coming from?" They wanted to know. They had never encountered anything like this before. The devil's kingdom was being shaken. Everywhere Yeshua went, he was able to establish the kingdom of God right in the middle of Satan's territory. Satan was losing control, and he knew it.

He anguished when he watched Yeshua stand over Peter's mother-in-law and rebuke her fever—caused by his spirit of infirmity—and saw it leave. Before Satan knew it, Yeshua was healing multitudes, laying hands on them and curing everyone. Satan was aghast when Yeshua cleansed the leper—first one, then two, and then a whole group of them at once. Fingers and limbs that had been eaten away mysteriously appeared where there had been none. *This was getting out of hand.*

It went on and on. The palsied were healed. The blind were restored to sight on more than one occasion. Paralyzed people walked, limbs that were withered were restored, and Yeshua seemed to be able to cure every disease of the multitudes that came to him.

Most disquieting were the numerous times when those who were controlled by unclean spirits were delivered, especially the demoniac of Gadara. He had been completely infested with demons. He was one of hell's prize specimens. Having been bound often with shackles for his feet and handcuffs made of chains for his hands, he had easily wrenched them apart. No one had strength enough to restrain him.

Night and day he roamed the graveyard on the mountainside, shrieking and screaming, beating and cutting himself with stones. Then Yeshua came along. Before they knew it, a whole legion of demons had been expelled, and the demoniac was in his right mind again. The demons all wound up in a herd of hogs, which they incited so thoroughly that they rushed headlong down the steep slope into the lake, drowned without a trace.

There were even times when Yeshua spoke a word only, and people in the grip of demonic spirits were delivered, and spirits of infirmity left the sick even when Yeshua was not present.

Report after report reached Satan's ears. The most disturbing news of all was the propaganda Yeshua was spreading among the masses.

"Love your enemies," he preached. "Forgive those who persecute you. Do good to those who despitefully use you."

If enough people started to believe that nonsense, there would be nobody that Satan's emissaries could control.

For three and a half years, Yeshua wrecked havoc in the curse-laden kingdom set up by hell. Frustrated at every turn, Satan resorted to stirring up the religious fanatics every chance he got. That still didn't stop Yeshua.

The event that sealed Satan's resolve occurred at the tomb of Lazarus. Death was Satan's specialty—his masterstroke. He had used one of his favorite means of destruction: the spirit of infirmity had struck Lazarus down with sickness. Yeshua had been so apathetic that he had let him die. The pain it had caused had been gratifying. Nevertheless, after four days, Yeshua stood at Lazarus's grave, and with just a command, the dead had been raised. That was startling to say the least. Now Satan knew for sure: Yeshua must be stopped at any cost.

This man who was causing the multitudes to chase after him, fawn all over him, and even worship him had to be wiped out before the entire world would follow suit. Satan's kingdom was in danger of being suppressed at the least, and if this madness wasn't curtailed, everything he had built up throughout the centuries would be completely destroyed.

A plan was beginning to formulate in Satan's devious mind. The ones most susceptible to demonic influence were the self-righteous Pharisees, the Sadducees, and scribes that continually hounded Yeshua everywhere he went. Sneaking around, they tried to catch Yeshua disobeying their rules in what he said or by his actions. Satan certainly could use them.

Then there was Judas. What could be better? A traitor right in the inner circle of those closest to Yeshua. Satan had Judas right in the palm of his hands. Judas was greedy; that would push him over the edge.

The stage was set. The time was right. But before he would have Yeshua killed, Satan's intention was to make it a slow, painful death with as much suffering as he could inflict on a human.

That could mean only one thing: *crucifixion*.

Chapter Sixteen

Sydney, Australia

John had barely gotten started reading the New Testament when he realized the light from his study window had dimmed so much that he could hardly see the words on the pages any more. He was already spent, not only from the events that had happened that morning, but his outburst at supper hadn't helped any. He was ashamed of himself. Sure, he was struggling with his opinion of the Almighty, but to hit Jeanne in the face with it…well, that was unacceptable.

He pulled his weary body from behind his desk and one by one lit the gas lanterns positioned around the room. *I wonder when we will ever be able to afford some electric lights like so many have already got? Probably never…as long as I am in this business of helping people, I'll always be poor.* John banged the door shut on the lantern. The light flickered and almost went out. His emotion was so forceful it was a wonder the glass lamp didn't tumble to the floor, broken.

John continued lighting the rest of the gas lights while mumbling to his self. "Just doesn't seem right. Them that carry on in the world get rich but those that work for God get poorer. It just doesn't seem fair somehow."

John was surprised at the negative thoughts swirling around in his mind. He had always been a positive person, excited to be privileged to do the Lord's work. Seeing one after the other of broken humanity come to Jesus and then become useful to society had been so fulfilling that he had never yearned much for worldly things.

But the struggle of the past few weeks had taken its toll. He was tired with a weariness that went far beyond the physical; it was a fatigue that reached to his very heart where joy had resided in the past, extinguishing it with a heavy burden of negativity.

John could hardly lift his head as he dropped into his chair. He had to find the answers. Where was God in all of this? He had just read about Jesus facing Satan in the wilderness. He could certainly identify with what Jesus had faced. His wilderness was every bit as bad as the one in the Scriptures—at least that's what he thought. Here in his desert there might be rain outside his window, but down on the inside—in his spirit—it was just as dry as where Jesus had been during his time of temptation.

John had noticed that the Almighty had not reached down his hand to remove Jesus from his time of testing, yet he had come out victorious. *Will I too get out of this victorious?* John buried his face in his hands. *Right now it doesn't look very promising...unless I get some answers.*

John knew that no matter how tired his body and spirit was, he had vowed to get some kind of understanding from God—no matter how long it took. He would have to press on in his search. John had just picked up his Bible and was thumbing through it to find the place where he had left off reading when he heard a knock on his study door.

"John, there is someone here to see you." John wasn't surprised to hear that Jeanne's voice was a little more timid than usual—considering his mood the last time they had spoken. Despite how John really felt on the inside, he tried to soften his tone when he answered.

"Send 'em in." John pushed back his chair as the door opened. Clancy Edwards came into the study with his hat held awkwardly in front of him.

"I…I needed to stop by, Pastor, to let you know what Emma and I are doing." Clancy cleared his throat as though a blockage was trying to strangle the words about to come out.

"Sure Clancy, have a seat." John gestured toward the lounge facing his desk—the only other piece of furniture in his tiny office.

Clancy perched on the edge of the lounge and twisted his hat round and round in his trembling hands. "Sarah's death was the last straw for us."

"I know; it was hard on all of us." John leaned forward as he tried to look in Clancy's eyes—eyes that were working hard at avoiding John's.

Besides being a deacon and one of the biggest givers in John's congregation, Clancy was John's friend. John had treasured the many hours they had spent together over tea discussing views of difficult Bible passages. They had fished together and even played an occasional game of rugby in the lane out back. But most of all, Clancy had been John's main encourager. Many times when he had gone through some of the numerous valleys of the ministry, Clancy had lifted him up. But this time, foreboding gripped John's already battered soul. What Clancy was about to tell him would be John's loss—that he was sure of.

"We're leavin', Pastor. There's too much death here." A sob slipped past Clancy's reserved exterior, punctuating his declaration. "We have to think about our family. You know how that disease works. It can be caught by just breathin' the air of them that are sick."

For the first time since entering John's study, Clancy's pleading eyes found John's. "You know how fast the plague could go through all eight of my kids. God could take all of them just like that."

The snap of Clancy's fingers sounded like the clang of a jail cell trapping its prisoner inside. John could feel the noose tightening around his mind. They were all captives of this dreaded scourge, unable to see their way out.

"I'm lookin' for answers." John pointed to his Bible. He hated the lack of conviction he heard in his voice.

"Well, you better get some soon, or we'll all be goners." Clancy stood as though he was ready to leave, but then he walked over in front of John. "You know Robert and Ellie's baby died this morning too."

"No…no." John shook his head. He leaned back in his chair and threw his hands heavenward. Then grasping the hair on the back of his head in tight fists, he glared at the ceiling. "God, where are you? When is all of this gonna stop?" He was almost shouting.

Clancy just hung his head in silence. John could see the grief in Clancy's face and the compassion that he had for his flock took over. He edged around the desk and threw his arm around his friend's shoulder. "I'm so sorry, mate. I know you cared a lot about that little one."

Even though John had never met Robert and Ellie, Clancy had talked in animated terms about his neighbors and had over and over mentioned their new baby as though it had been one of his own. Clancy couldn't hold back the sobs any longer. His manly pride dissolved as he clung to John as if a hurricane were about to rip him away to an unknown place of destruction.

After a moment of allowing the sobs to come unhindered, Clancy pulled away from John's embrace. He pulled out a hanky from his back pocket and blew his nose. "Find the answer, Pastor. You gotta find the answer." He gave John a long, searching look then turned and stumbled out the door, eyes straight ahead.

As the study door clicked shut, John turned once again to the book laying open on his desk. *Is the answer really in this book?* John shook his head. *It has to be. It just has to be. Where else can I turn? If the answer is not in the Bible, then I guess all hope is lost.*

As the curtain of night settled over the sorrowing countryside, John began to journey through the pages of the gospels alongside a suffering Christ who had brought light into a world filled with darkness.

Part Three

Chapter Seventeen

Jerusalem at Passover

Controversy swirled around Yeshua like a cyclone. It threatened to alter the religious landscape of his day by uprooting the deep-seated beliefs of multitudes throughout Galilee and the regions of Judea. The Sanhedrin was alarmed. Change didn't set well with these seventy ruling elders of the Jewish religious community.

Yeshua had emerged from the wilderness filled with the Holy Spirit, consumed with compassion for the oppressed masses of humanity. Fueled by the urgency to reach as many as he could with the good news of the kingdom of God, Yeshua had maintained a constant flurry of ministry. Everywhere he went, signs and wonders and miracles and extraordinary deliverances followed. Thousands of enthusiasts had championed his cause. The majority of his followers were made up of ordinary people, but every once in a while, men and women of social status would join with him.

Out of the many that followed him, Yeshua had chosen twelve who made up the company that stayed close by his side throughout the three and a half years of his ministry. As widespread as his popularity had become, and even though the results had been spectacular, Yeshua knew his real mission was yet to be fulfilled.

Yes, he had demonstrated his Father's will over sickness and disease. Certainly, he had wielded his God-given authority over demons and even death. Nevertheless, he knew the greatest challenge was just ahead. The power that flowed so easily through his hands must be deposited into the lives of mortal men. But how could a sinful man take dominion over Satan's kingdom? It could never be. That meant sin had to be dealt with.

He was the Lamb of God sent to take away the sins of the world. His time had come.

Yeshua was quite aware that the agitation of the Jewish leaders had mushroomed throughout the city of Jerusalem. However, that had not stopped him from wreaking havoc with the moneychanger's despicable trade a few days before. He had been just plain angry at their utter disregard for his Father's house. Some would probably say he had been a little overly zealous, but he didn't think so.

"It is written," Yeshua had cried, "'My house shall be called a house of prayer for all the nations, but you have made it a den of robbers.'"

There in the Court of the Gentiles, he had made a whip of cords and overturned the tables where they changed money along with toppling the seats of the merchants who sold pigeons. He had also stopped those who were using the temple courts as a shortcut for carrying goods from one section of Jerusalem to another.

When he had left the city that evening to return to Bethany, he knew there would be a serious consultation among the religious leaders about what he had done.

So be it, Yeshua thought as he headed back to Jerusalem the next morning with his disciples.

As they crested the brow of the Mount of Olives, they paused at the magnificent sight that lay before them. Sprawled out on the heights across the Kidron Valley, the glorious city created by Herod the Great came into view. White stones of the temple embellished with gold filigree gleamed in the bright Palestinian sun; its beauty could be seen for miles away. All around the temple mount, splendid marble porticos graced the massive retaining walls—walls that had been built out of large beautifully dressed ashlar stones.

As stunning as the city was that sparkled in all of its elegance, Yeshua could only see a place destined for destruction. Sorrow was etched on his features as tears gathered in his eyes. His love for the population caused his heart to constrict in anguish at the perils that lay ahead for them.

"O Jerusalem, Jerusalem," he cried. "You who kill the prophets and stone those who are sent to you. How often I have yearned to gather your children together around me as a hen gathers her young under her wings, but you would not."

Andrew, who was standing closest to Yeshua, overheard the heartrending pronouncement. A confused expression flashed across his face as he turned to Peter who was hurrying up the hill ahead of the other disciples. He gave Peter a look that said, "I wonder what he's talking about?"

Both shrugged their shoulders. Sadness on the countenance of their leader always made them uncomfortable. Normally, Yeshua was in high spirits to say the least—even jovial at times. But over the last few days, Yeshua had appeared more somber and reflective than usual. The disciples had become more and more concerned about his safety. They noticed he didn't seem to mind that he had offended, on more than one occasion, not only the Jewish leaders, but also some of his followers.

"Rabbi, you know the Jews were incensed about what happened with the moneychangers. Do you really think it's wise to go back into the city today?" Andrew asked.

Yeshua turned and grasped each of Andrew's shoulders. Looking deep into his eyes with an expression that hinted at mysteries that only the rabbi knew, Yeshua spoke with a voice pregnant with hidden meaning, "I must continue on my way today and tomorrow and the day after that, for it will never do for a prophet to be destroyed away from Jerusalem."

The disciples glanced at one another with unspoken questions in their eyes.

"Yeshua has been talking about death a lot lately," James whispered in John's ear. "I don't like the sound of it."

"Neither do I," John muttered. "With what he did to the moneychangers, those religious folks are going to be mighty mad. All those people crammed into the city for the Passover, it's a hotbed for trouble."

Thomas tugged on Peter's sleeve and then leaned his head close to Peter's. "Can't you persuade Yeshua not to go into Jerusalem today? We could prepare for the Passover feast in Bethany." Thomas gestured in the direction from which they had come. "It would be less dangerous."

Thomas wrung his hands and then gave Peter a slight nudge toward Yeshua. "Find out where we are going to celebrate the feast. Does he even know anyone here in Jerusalem that has a place we can use?"

Peter edged up to Yeshua's side. Clearing his throat, he asked, "Master, where do you want us to go and prepare the Passover supper for you to eat?"

Peter fidgeted as he waited almost a full minute for Yeshua to answer. Then just as Peter was about ready to ask the question again, Yeshua said, "Go into the city, and a man carrying an earthen pitcher of water will meet you; follow him. Whatever house he enters, tell the master of the house that the teacher would like to use his guest room to eat the Passover supper with his disciples."

Noticing that John had stepped up beside Peter, Yeshua put his arm around his shoulder and pointing to Peter, said, "You go along with Peter. When you find the man, he will show you a large upper room furnished with carpets and dining couches that will be spread and ready; there, prepare the room for us. Not only will it be ready for tomorrow's feast, but we will partake of supper there tonight."

Peter and John both knew what preparing the room for the Passover feast meant. Since it was also the first day of the Feast of Unleavened Bread, it was customary to make the house ready where the Feast of the Passover was to be held by removing any trace of leavening—or *chametz*—from the premises. The consumption of *chametz* was forbidden during Passover. So this required a meticulous search in every corner and crevice using candlelight to illuminate the areas. With a feather to dust out the hidden places, every spot had to be swept clean before the place was considered *kosher* for the feast.

The two disciples hurried across the Kidron Valley and disappeared through the Susa gate that led to Solomon's porch. From there, they proceeded into the upper city of Jerusalem to follow Yeshua's instructions.

Yeshua waited for an hour or two on the hillside. He reclined on the grassy slope before continuing toward the gates of Jerusalem with the rest of his disciples who followed reluctantly behind. On the way, they quietly deliberated among themselves about the events of the last few days and how unconcerned Yeshua seemed about the possible consequences of opposing the religious system. There was no doubt they were nervous.

Yeshua and the disciples crossed the Kidron Valley. As they entered the golden gate that led to the courtyard surrounding the temple, Peter and John came rushing to meet them.

"It happened just like you said," puffed Peter, trying to catch his breath.

"You should see the house," John said with eyes big with excitement. "It has a courtyard and baths for cleansing and trees; everything was already prepared before we got there."

"Come. Come, we'll show you where it is." Peter grabbed Yeshua's hand and started pulling him toward the western gate behind the temple.

"There is no hurry." Yeshua stopped Peter by grasping his other hand. "We have plenty of time." Yeshua let his gaze follow the multitudes of people swarming the plaza—families with children, businessmen selling their wares, and soldiers mingling with the common peasants ready to keep order should a disturbance arise. Here and there were rabbis and priests dressed in their religious garments, directing the travelers to various parts of the temple mount. Yeshua's heart ached for the masses that seemed to have no joy and no direction—sheep without a shepherd.

The courtyard was choked with pilgrims pushing and shoving their way through the many entrances to the temple grounds. Travelers poured in from the Joppa road through the Western gate and from roads that led into the city from other directions. Many were leading or carrying spring lambs to sacrifice for the Feast of the Passover that was to begin the following day.

As Yeshua and his disciples jostled their way through the temple courtyard, they were surrounded by the constant commotion of voices contending to be heard above the throng. The clatter of hooves on the smooth stone pavement of the plaza added to the tumult. Odors of cooking food drifted throughout the temple area carried about on the breezes that blew from the tent city outside the gates erected to accommodate the thousands of pilgrims who had come to Jerusalem for the Passover feast.

Yeshua and his disciples zigzagged across the Court of the Gentiles and through the Royal Porch that surrounded the temple area. The crowd began to thin somewhat as they made their way out the southernmost gate. After they crossed the bridge spanning the aqueduct that divided the city down the middle, the upper city came into view.

The houses there were spacious for the most part and built by the wealthier segment of the population. Rich and powerful Jewish families and high-ranking Roman officials had erected elegant, white marble mansions around courtyards with elaborate gardens and pools.

The broad, fashionable avenues of the upper city were laid out in an orderly grid pattern, unlike the maze of dusty streets and alleyways running in every direction in the lower city where the common laborers lived.

Yeshua could feel the icy glare of some of the Jewish leaders as they walked past the open court of the high priest's palace. They continued up the narrow street that led to the interior of the city, and there they came to a courtyard that surrounded a complex of structures made out of stones plastered with stucco and covered with artistic frescoes.

The house was not one built by the wealthiest of the upper class in Jerusalem, nor was it a one-story dwelling typical of the working people. However, it was constructed of cut stones, which only the well-to-do could afford. A five-foot wall surrounded the courtyard that was graced with stately sycamore and olive trees. Within the courtyard were three separate buildings. In the western corner was a stable, and across a smaller courtyard stood two buildings side by side, one of which was two stories high with a stone stairway leading up to an arched entrance.

Yeshua and the disciples followed Peter and John as they mounted the steps to the upper guest chamber. The room was just as John had described. In the center was a table with dishes and cups already set with matzo and wine, various kinds of cheeses, an assortment of vegetables, and dates, and at one end sat a large mound of grapes. Surrounding the table on all sides were positioned thirteen couches for reclining.

The disciples bumped into each other as they tried to claim the best place at the table, disputing loudly about who deserved to sit where. Finally, Phillip, who always seemed to be the take-charge diplomat, was able to establish some kind of order. When the disciples were satisfied with the arrangements, they finally proceeded with the meal.

Yeshua did not say a word throughout the main part of supper but ate quietly, deep in thought. He was fully aware that the time had come for him to leave this world and return to the Father. Weighing on his mind was the revelation that his heavenly Father had put everything into his hands. He was aware that soon he would transfer that authority into the hands of the very ones who sat at the table with him, including those who would subsequently believe in him for centuries to come.

He looked at each of his disciples: Peter and Andrew, brothers who were boisterous and impulsive, yet their leadership ability was unmistakable; James and John, who were well named Sons of Thunder because of their quick tempers and brusque dispositions, still they had hearts as big as Mount Hermon; and there was Philip the peacemaker, and beside him sat Thomas who was too intellectual for his own good—always had to analyze the deep meaning of things.

On the right of Thomas sat Bartholomew. One couldn't help but like his congenial manner, and by his side was Matthew—in the past, a tax collector hated by the Jews, but now a level-headed colleague. Leaning over to converse with Matthew was his brother James of Alphaeus, who always had an opinion about everything. It was hard for James to believe that there was any other way of doing a job except his way.

At the end of the table sat Simon Zelotes, who was quick to champion the cause of the underdog, and at the other end was Thaddeus—quiet and good-natured with a dry sense of humor. Then there was Judas Iscariot—well, Yeshua knew what was ahead for him. Yeshua's heart ached.

How he loved all of them. As imperfect as they were, he loved them to the highest degree. Earlier, Yeshua had observed their bickering for the best position at the table. Their heated discussion as to who was the greatest among them had reached his ears. Although he had shown no indication that he had heard, right then, he decided this would be a good time to teach them a valuable lesson in humility, considering the time was drawing near when he would leave this world.

Yeshua was aware that soon these very men would be endowed with the authority of the kingdom of Heaven. It was vital that that authority be exercised with humility. Not like the Gentiles who routinely lorded it over their subjects, ruling them with tyranny. It must not be so among his followers. Yes, they were to rule with power over Satan and his kingdom—but not over people.

The low murmur of conversation among the disciples halted as Yeshua arose from the table. Their eyes followed his movement with curiosity as he deliberately removed his outer garments and picked up a servant's towel that was lying beside a washbasin and fastened it around his waist. Since the servants who had prepared the supper had already departed before they had gotten there, no one in their group had offered to fill that role when they had arrived.

Sheepish expressions registered on the countenances of the disciples as Yeshua poured water into the basin and commenced to wash their feet one by one. Judas's face flushed when Yeshua purposely knelt and gently bathed his feet while holding his gaze with a look of sadness.

When Yeshua had finished with the last disciple, he wiped his hands on the towel, pulled on his outer cloak once again, and said, "You may not understand now what I have done, but you will understand later on."

Then reclining once again on the couch at the table, he leaned his elbow on the table and addressed the bewildered group who stared silently in his direction. "I have given you this example so you will act in the same manner as I have done to you. I most solemnly tell you that a servant is not greater than his master, and no one who is sent is superior to the one who sent him. As my Father has appointed a kingdom and conferred it on me, so do I confer on you the privileges and the decree."

Yeshua then placed both hands on the table as he leaned forward. His expression equaled the sternness in his voice. "Whoever desires to be great among you must be your servants. Just as I, the Son of man, came not to be waited on but to serve."

The disciples avoided each other's eyes as each one focused on random spots on the opposite wall. They squirmed on their couches as though they were being harassed by insects. But Judas appeared to be the most uncomfortable of all, especially when Yeshua turned toward him, staring intently in his direction.

No one spoke. In fact, the duly reprimanded group hardly breathed as the silence stretched on for several minutes. Abruptly, Yeshua broke the stillness. "He who eats bread with me has raised up his heel against me."

The disciples looked at one another puzzled. Yeshua was quoting from the psalms, but why? Judas studied his fingernails.

A cloud seemed to have descended upon Yeshua's countenance as he continued. "Most solemnly, I tell you that one of you will betray me."

At that surprise pronouncement, the disciples began to whisper among themselves. Peter elbowed John, who was closest to Yeshua, motioning for him to ask Yeshua who he was talking about. John hesitated for a second then leaned over to Yeshua. "Whom are you referring to, Lord?" he asked.

"It is the one to whom I am going to give this morsel of food after I have dipped it." Resolutely, Yeshua broke off a piece of bread and sopped it in the dish that sat in front of him. Judas appeared flustered as Yeshua leaned across the table and handed him the bread. Judas's eyes widened as he took the portion. A confused look registered on his countenance for only a second, but then a hardened expression twisted his features into a determined look.

Yeshua watched the evidence of the inward struggle take place inside the disciple. As Judas's visage darkened, Yeshua shook his head sadly and said, "What you are going to do, make quick work of it."

Judas dropped the morsel on the table as though it were a burning piece of coal and immediately went out into the gathering darkness. The battle for his soul was over. The choice had been made, and Satan had won. The hour had come, and the power of darkness would have its way.

Chapter Eighteen

Judas's abrupt departure drew only a passing notice from the other eleven men. None had paid close enough attention to Yeshua's hurried announcement of impending betrayal to afterward connect it with what had transpired between Judas and Yeshua. Judas was noted for being a cauldron of activity. He insisted on carrying the purse that contained funds for the ministry, so he was always coming and going while taking care of the financial obligations that arose, also giving money to the poor when Yeshua directed.

Yeshua's attention stayed riveted on the door through which Judas had exited until footsteps could no longer be heard. When he faced the remaining disciples once again, there was a look of intensity about him that stopped all conversation at the table. The discourse that followed would be long remembered for its poignant content and the urgency with which it was given.

Yeshua stood once again and picked up the matzo from the center of the table. Lifting it toward heaven, Yeshua recited the beginning of the Haggadah as he gave thanks. "Blessed are you, O Lord Jehovah, King of the universe, the Creator who brings forth bread from the earth."

Yeshua broke off pieces of the bread and handed them to each of the disciples. "Take and eat," he said. "This is my body which is given for you. Do this in remembrance of me."

Each of the men solemnly ate as they were instructed. But the glances they gave each other suggested questions were whirling through their minds. From their expressions, it was evident they were remembering another sermon Yeshua had taught only a few days before when so many of Yeshua's followers had become offended.

"Eat his flesh," the multitude had ridiculed the thought. "Who can be expected to listen to such teaching?"

Nevertheless, the disciples had continued to trust Yeshua. He explained that it was spiritual things he had been referring to, not his literal flesh. Now, they could understand that eating the bread was a representation of his body, just as eating a covenant meal symbolized becoming one with a covenant partner. A covenant with Jehovah's representative had to be a good thing.

Next, Yeshua picked up the cup of wine. Cupping his hands around it, he held it out toward his attentive audience. Hesitating momentarily, he bowed his head slightly and closed his eyes for a few seconds as a look of anguish flickered across his face. Then lifting his eyes once again, his focus moved from one face to another. "This is my blood of the new covenant, which ratifies the agreement and is being poured out for many to obtain forgiveness of sins. Drink of it, all of you."

A blood covenant—the disciples could understand that concept. Blood represented the life of a person or an animal. When a lamb was sacrificed—such as the *korban pesach,* which was offered during Passover—its blood was offered on the altar, signifying a life given to cover the sins of the worshipper. Because the person who sins must die, then the innocent lamb's life was a substitute for the life of the sinner. The sinner could then go free, made righteous by the blood of the lamb. However, this had to be done yearly to cover all the sins committed during that period of time. Any good son of Abraham knew if that sacrifice were not made, he would no longer be in good standing as a covenant partner with Yahweh.

Yeshua realized these eleven men would not fully comprehend now the significance of what they had just done, but later, in just a few more days, full understanding would come. And through them, ultimately, the whole world would know. Heaven was counting on it.

After each disciple had drunk from the cup, Yeshua continued, "Now is the Son of man glorified. I will be with you only a little while longer; you will not be able to come with me."

"Lord, where are you going?" Peter interrupted.

Yeshua didn't answer his question but said instead, "You cannot follow me now where I am going, but you will follow me afterward."

"But, Lord, why can't I follow you now?" Peter asked. "You know I would lay down my life for you."

Yeshua laid his hand on Peter's shoulder. As he answered him, the timbre in his voice revealed the fondness he had for this rough, outspoken disciple.

"Simon, Simon, Satan has asked that you be given over to him out of the power and keeping of Jehovah so that he might sift you like wheat."

Then giving Peter's shoulder an affectionate squeeze, he added, "But I have prayed for you that your faith will not fail. Afterward, when it is all over, you will be able to strengthen and establish your brethren."

"Lord, I am ready to go with you both to prison and even to death." Peter's passion was unmistakable.

Yeshua shook his head sorrowfully. "Peter, before a single cock shall crow this day, you will three times deny that you know me."

Before Peter could protest that statement, Yeshua continued to address the rest of the disciples who sat listening intently. He gave them a new commandment to love one another, which would fulfill the letter of the law—a love that would define them as his disciples. He told them about his Father's house where there were mansions being prepared for them. In-depth instruction was given about the Holy Spirit that was to come to indwell them—his character, his function, and his role in empowering them in prayer and ministry.

As the supper concluded, Yeshua drew his teaching to a close by saying, "Peace I bequeath to you. Not as the world gives, give I you. Don't let your heart be troubled and afraid. Yes, I am going away, but if you really loved me, you would be glad because I am going to the Father, and he is greater and mightier than I am."

Then, as they prepared to leave the upper room, Yeshua led them in a hymn. When they finished singing, they remained with heads bowed for a short period of time in reverence, sensing the remarkable presence of Jehovah that had filled the room.

Then softly, Yeshua broke the silence. "The evil ruler of this world is coming, but he has nothing in common with me. There is nothing in me that belongs to him, and he has no power over me. Nevertheless, he is coming, and I will do what my Father has commanded me so that the world may know that I love the Father and that I act in full agreement with his orders."

Yeshua slowly arose from his reclining position and motioned to his disciples. "Arise," he said. "Let us go away from here."

Holding torches for illumination, Yeshua and the eleven men made their way back down to the street. Meandering along the road that passed in front of the large theater built by Herod, they continued up the avenue alongside the Hasmonean Palace and once again entered the temple area. Pushing their way through the still-crowded Court of the Gentiles, they exited through the golden gate. Crossing the Kidron Valley over the bridge that spanned the torrent of cascading water running through the valley from the winter's downpour, they approached the entrance of the Garden of Gethsemane, located at the base of the Mount of Olives.

All along the way, Yeshua had taken advantage of those last few minutes of time with his disciples to talk further with them about the Holy Spirit. He also warned them of the persecution they were going to face because of their belief in him.

By the time they reached the garden, the sun had completely disappeared behind the horizon. The night chill had set in, causing the disciples to gather their cloaks more tightly around their bodies for added warmth. The torches that illuminated the temple courts and the fires from the tents scattered outside the city walls cast a glow on the evening sky that lessened the intensity of the darkness on the hillside.

The disciples were familiar with this area. Yeshua had led them here often, and many times he had come to this spot alone to pray. Even in the dusk, the large, overhanging trees were still visibly outlined against the evening glow as though forming a canopy of seclusion from the invading darkness. Here and there were huge, twisted tree trunks evidence of the ravages of nature and the unrelenting passage of time.

Yeshua leaned against one of the stumps as his disciples gathered around him. He motioned for them to be seated, and then as the night deepened, he gave them his final instructions. A holy radiance lit up Yeshua's countenance as he looked into the upturned faces he had grown so familiar with over the last three and half years. He knew their pasts—just ordinary men. In the world's eyes, uneducated and uncouth, hardly worth taking note of. But he also knew their future. They would turn the world upside down. They would change the world.

"From now on, you shall not need to ask me anything." Yeshua's voice pierced the darkness. "I assure you that my Father will grant you whatever you ask in my name. Ask, and you shall receive that your joy may be full and complete."

Yeshua stopped for a moment to clear his throat. He could feel a lump that refused to allow him to continue. Moisture gathered in his eyes as love for these men overwhelmed his emotions. And not love for them alone. Love for all humanity gripped his heart so tightly that it threatened to cause it to burst with the passion of it.

When Yeshua could finally speak again, the words came heavy with emotion. "The Father tenderly loves you because you have loved me and believe that I have come from him. I came out from my Father into this world; now I am leaving the world and am going back to the Father."

"Ah, now you are speaking plainly to us and not in veiled language." Yeshua recognized the voice as belonging to James of

Alpheus. "Now we know that you know everything. Because of this, we believe that you really did come from God."

Yeshua could faintly make out the other's heads shaking in agreement with James's admission.

"Do you now believe? Do you believe it at last?" Yeshua felt a great weight lift from his shoulders. This was what he wanted to hear from his disciples before he was taken away from them. His many hours of teaching had not been in vain. The course was now complete. They were ready.

"I have told you these things so in me you can have perfect peace and confidence. In the world, it is not going to be easy. You will face tribulation and trials. At times, you will experience distress and frustration. But be of good courage for I have overcome the world. I have deprived it of power to harm you. I have conquered it for you."

Then having spoken those things, Yeshua lifted up his eyes to heaven and prayed one final prayer over his devoted followers who had left so much to stand by his side.

"Father, the hour has come. Glorify and exalt your son, so that I may honor you. I have glorified you down here on the earth by completing the work that you have given me to do."

Then stretching out his hands toward his disciples, Yeshua continued, "My Father, I pray for these you have given to me that they may be one even as we are one so that the world may be convinced that you have sent me and know that you have loved them even as you have loved me."

Yeshua paused for a moment as he looked down through the centuries to come at the vast multitudes that would someday believe on him. Joy flooded his soul at the thought.

Then he continued, "I am coming to you, but I pray that these, my disciples, will be filled with my joy and that they will have my gladness within them filling their hearts."

Yeshua lifted his hands as he became more aware of the glory of his Father and the presence of unseen beings from the heavenly realm. "Oh, just and righteous Father, I have given to them the glory and honor, which you have given me. Just as you sent me into the world, I now also send them into the world. I have made your name known to them and revealed your character that the love which you have bestowed upon me may be in them."

Having concluded the prayer, the disciples sat without moving a muscle. Quietness prevailed in the garden. In the distance, the cry of a child and the murmur of conversation traveled on the breeze, but no sound came from the men seated there. They spoke not a word, completely overwhelmed by the power and significance of what had just transpired, awed by the overpowering sense of the destiny that lay ahead for them.

Yeshua too knew what awaited him in the coming hours. He had been born for this moment, but now that it had come, how could he bear it? Yes, he was going back to be with his Father; but what he would have to go through before then—the horror of it came crushing down upon him.

Chapter Nineteen

Darkness closed in on Yeshua like a suffocating blanket. Not the kind of blackness that comes in the dead of night, but a dimming of light in the soul that threatens to extinguish even the most powerful illumination. Time after time, Yeshua had spoken of his death, even identifying the type of death it would be. Now that the time had come, death stood in front of him, leering, impatient, and foreboding.

It was not physical death that Yeshua dreaded most in spite of the horrendous suffering it would inflict on his body. No, what Yeshua shrank from was the spiritual death that awaited him. The cup handed to him by his Father was filled with the sins of the world—past, present, and future; a cup so evil and so ghastly that his righteous soul recoiled at the thought.

After Yeshua had finished praying for the disciples, he knew he must now pray for himself. The presence of Jehovah had lifted from the disciples, leaving them fatigued and drained emotionally. One by one they stretched out on the ground in relaxed positions, preparing to fall asleep.

"You stay here," Yeshua addressed the group as a whole, "while I go over yonder to pray." The disciples could barely see Yeshua by the light of the few torches they had planted in the ground as he pointed toward the more dense area of the garden.

Yeshua turned toward Peter, James, and John who were positioned side by side absorbed in conversation. There was a noticeable slump in Yeshua's shoulders and hollowness in his voice as he spoke directly to them.

"Would you three come with me?"

The three disciples quickly jumped to their feet, grabbed a torch, and followed Yeshua farther into the garden. When they came to a place where the shrubbery and foliage formed a natural secluded area, Yeshua came to a stop.

Dropping his face into his hands, he shook his head from side to side. "My soul is very sad and deeply grieved so that I am almost dying of sorrow."

Agony was written all over his face as he lifted his eyes to the three men. "Stay here and keep awake and watch with me."

Yeshua stumbled on into the night about a stone's throw away. He threw himself upon the ground on his face and began to travail.

"Abba, if it is possible, let this cup pass from me."

Inside, Yeshua was being ripped in two directions. On one hand, he could see lost humanity who had chosen to drink of the cup of sin. Their lives had been battered by the curse that sin had released in the earth. Hatred had goaded men and women to cruelty toward their fellow man, while wicked, malevolent spirits had driven mankind to perform every kind of immoral act. Like a tumultuous sea seething under the influence of hurricane force winds, the human race had been whipped to a frenzy by the brutal rule of Satan's blasphemous kingdom. Compassion for Adam's race pulled on Yeshua's heart until he felt as though it would literally break apart.

On the other hand, Yeshua knew what it would mean to drink of the cup being offered him. Sin had not once touched his spirit. The shame and humiliation of its consequences had never tarnished his soul. He had never experienced the oppression of the spirit of infirmity crippling his human body with sickness or disease. Guilt had never interfered with his relationship with his heavenly Father.

Yet Yeshua knew if he accepted the iniquitous cup, he would become the greatest sinner of all. He who knew no sin would become sin itself. Like all the rest of Adam's race, he, Yeshua, would come under the control of the ruler of darkness, his archenemy: Satan himself. The idea was repulsive. His heart was crushed at the very thought of it.

The struggle was so severe that Yeshua began to perspire from the intensity of the battle. He felt as though his life was being sucked from his body. He lay on the ground as one dead. After a few minutes, Yeshua stirred and finally forced himself to his knees. Turning his face heavenward, he let out a guttural cry, "Adoni…not my will…but your will be done."

As soon as those heart-wrenching words left his lips, Yeshua felt the hand of an angel rest upon his head. The sweet breath of life sent from heaven poured into his mortal body. Feeling somewhat invigorated once again, Yeshua rose to his feet. The battle was not over. He knew that much. He looked around to find the angel, but he had disappeared. Yeshua did not want to go through this struggle alone. He needed to know someone else was helping him in this conflict.

Yeshua went back to where he had left Peter, James, and John. Expecting to find them in prayer, he was disappointed to discover they were sound asleep. As he observed the three sprawled out on the ground, unaware of the spiritual warfare raging all around, he was grieved. Sure, their flesh needed rest, but what they would experience before this night was over required them to be strong in the spirit and in the power of Jehovah's might. Prayer was what would strengthen the spirit.

Yeshua shook each one of them until they came to a sitting position. Rubbing their eyes, they squinted at the shadowy form of Yeshua. As he spoke, they jumped at the sternness of his voice.

"What! Are you unable to stay awake and watch with me for only one hour?"

He looked from one to the other with concern etched on his countenance. "All of you, you must stay awake. Watch and pray that you may not come into temptation."

Yeshua turned to go then whirled back around and added, "The spirit indeed is willing, but the flesh is weak."

When Yeshua arrived at the spot where he had prayed before, once again, he fell on his knees and with his face to the ground wrestled in prayer. "Abba, everything is possible for you; take away this cup from me."

The cup loomed before him, erupting with the stench of hell. Depraved and twisted, overflowing with the filth of centuries of demonic pleasures, Yeshua could not find the strength to embrace it—not yet.

The warfare was taking its toll. Yeshua could feel it. Nevertheless, again he affirmed his submission to his Father's will.

For the second time, Yeshua went back to check on his three disciples. They had tried to stay awake, but their eyes became too heavy. Before they knew it, they had fallen back to sleep. When Yeshua awakened them again, they didn't know what answer to give him. Yeshua warned them yet again of the danger of yielding to their flesh. Counseling them once more to use the hour ahead to pray, Yeshua for the third time went back to his place of prayer.

This time, the agony of his mind was practically unbearable. Sweat poured from his body like great clots of blood dropping upon the ground. The pressure caused his heart to feel as though it would explode. No human could bear this kind of burden for long and continue to live.

This time, Yeshua prayed even more earnestly. "Is there no other way except I drink of this cup? If it is at all possible, Abba Father, let this fatal hour pass from me."

As Yeshua lay on the ground battered and exhausted, a tiny speck of light floated up from his spirit, illuminating his mind. *I have come to take away the sins of the world. There is no other way. No alternate plan.* The thought penetrated his understanding.

He remembered what he had been taught about the sin offering from the book of the Law. Not one goat, but two would have to be brought to the high priest. One was to be slain to atone for the sins and transgressions of the people. Once killed, its blood was sprinkled on the mercy seat of the ark of the covenant. There,

Jehovah would view the blood of the sin offering and forgive their sins.

However, there was also a second goat—the scapegoat. The high priest would lay hands on it and confess the sins of the people on the head of that goat. Then, the scapegoat would be taken to the wilderness and loosed into a land not inhabited, carrying with it the sins of the people.

Yeshua remembered the common practice associated with the scapegoat was to tie a red strip of cloth to the goat. According to the Jewish Talmud, this red stripe would eventually turn white. Skeptics reasoned that the cloth was simply bleached white by the sun's rays but the Jews believed that it was a supernatural act of Jehovah signaling the fact that the punishment for sins had been paid.

Redemption had to be twofold. The justice of heaven must be satisfied by the sacrificed blood of an innocent lamb. But the battle for earth's authority had to be won in the wilderness in the bowels of hell itself. The originator of all sin—Satan himself—must be defeated in his own territory.

If he, Yeshua, paid the full penalty for the sins of the whole world, Satan would no longer have the legal right to rule over mankind. For that to happen, Yeshua would have to suffer the fate of the damned and come out victorious.

Satan might be successful in bruising my heel through crucifixion, Yeshua thought, *but in the end, I will crush his head. What a brilliant plan!*

The battle was over. Yeshua had made his decision. It was finally settled once and for all. It was as though the light of a thousand suns burst through Yeshua's soul. The cup that was being held out to him might be filled with the curses of humanity in the beginning, but in the end, it would become a cup of blessing.

Yeshua jumped to his feet. Yes, yes, he would embrace the cup. With a heart fully surrendered to his Father's will, Yeshua lifted his hands to heaven and with a strong, clear voice, declared, "Father, not my will, but yours be done."

In that moment, the fate of mankind was decided. All beings in heaven applauded, and Jehovah smiled as a single tear fell from his eye.

Chapter Twenty

The stillness that settled upon the garden of Gethsemane reached the depths of Yeshua's soul as strength flooded the battered edges of his emotions. He was ready—no, even eager to face the worst Satan had to offer. He didn't have long to wait. Yeshua could hear the scramble of numerous feet charging toward him. In the distance amid pinpoints of lights, he could detect the babble of voices conversing in hushed tones.

Yeshua stood still and waited. Minutes passed as the noise of the mob drew closer; Yeshua remained motionless. Already he could feel the hot breath of Satan panting in wild anticipation at what lay ahead. Yeshua couldn't help but smile. He was on the verge of stepping into his archenemy's well-laid trap, but in reality, the one who would in the end be ensnared would be Satan himself.

A holy anointing overwhelmed Yeshua as he calmly made his way back to where he had left Peter, James, and John.

"Still sleeping?" He gave Peter's shoulder a gentle shake. "Wake up. Look, the time has come. I, the Son of man, am betrayed into the hands of sinners."

Peter stretched and rubbed his eyes. As he tried to focus on the figure that stood before him, James and John stirred and then abruptly sat up.

"Up, all of you." Yeshua addressed the threesome in a commanding voice edged with just a hint of urgency. "We must be going. See, my betrayer is here."

As if on cue, Judas crashed into the clearing, followed by a band of soldiers carrying swords and clubs along with temple guards sent from the high priest and Pharisees holding lanterns and blazing torches.

They halted unceremoniously as they caught sight of Yeshua and his disciples illuminated in the dim light. Moments before, seasoned soldiers, who had built their careers on apprehending enraged fugitives, had stampeded relentlessly through the olive grove focused intently on capturing their victim. Now, in the presence of the one they had been so engrossed in overtaking, they stood frozen in place, disoriented and hesitant. Before them stood an ordinary-looking man, tranquil and poised, but emanating a power that confused and immobilized them.

No one spoke or made a sound for a short space of time. Then the impasse was broken as Yeshua stepped forward to meet them. "Who are you looking for?"

Soldiers looked at each other as though they had become suddenly mute. After a short wait, Malchus, the servant of the high priest, spoke up.

"Uh…we're looking for…uh…Jesus of Nazareth." He glanced out of the corner of his eye at the congregation of soldiers standing close beside him. Then, he glared at Judas, who had fallen back into the crowd, urging him forward with a slight nod of the head.

"I am he," Yeshua said without hesitation.

As the words *I am* left his mouth, a power accompanied those words unlike any band of soldiers had ever faced. A tangible force struck as though invisible hands had lifted them up and flung them backward to the ground.

For just an instant, the mound of tangled militia lay at Yeshua's feet. Yeshua stifled a chuckle as he watched the representatives of the highest authority in the land try to regain dignity as they scrambled to their feet. One by one, they straightened askew helmets and headgear while trying to look official.

Once more, Yeshua asked them, "Who are you looking for?"

This time, a chorus of voices answered back, "Jesus of Nazareth."

"I told you; I am he," Yeshua said. "And since I am the one you want, let these others go." He pointed in the direction of Peter, James, and John. He was aware that the other eight disciples were cowering in the shadows just a short distance behind them.

Still, the soldiers hesitated. They had orders to do nothing until the prearranged signal had been given.

"You will know which one to arrest when I go over and give him the kiss of greeting," Judas had told them.

They were waiting on Judas, but he had fallen back behind one of the tallest soldiers. Finally, one of the temple guards gave him a shove, and Judas found himself facing his mentor and friend. Hesitating for only a second, he hurried to Yeshua's side.

"Teacher!" he exclaimed a little too loudly. Then he embraced Yeshua and kissed him soundly on the cheek.

Yeshua grasped Judas shoulders and gazed sorrowfully into his eyes. In a voice that was barely audible, he said, "My friend, go ahead and do what you have come for."

That was the signal the soldiers had been waiting for. Pandemonium exploded all around as guards and soldiers surged forward, tripping over one another to make the arrest. They were preparing to chain Yeshua's hands when without warning, Peter jumped from behind Yeshua, wildly swinging a sword. Before Yeshua could stop him, he had taken aim at Malchus's head, intending to decapitate him; however, in the split second that Peter swung, Malchus ducked. The sword narrowly missed his head but slashed off his left ear, leaving it barely hanging by the tiniest sliver of flesh.

Yeshua grabbed Peter's arm, forcing him to stop his madness. "Put away your sword."

Yeshua jerked Peter up in front of him so he could address him face-to-face. "Those who live by the sword will die by the sword."

Then Yeshua motioned heavenward with his free hand. "Don't you realize that I could ask my Father for thousands of angels to protect us, and he would send them instantly?"

Yeshua loosed his hold on Peter's arm. His sword clattered to the ground. "But if I did, how then would the Scriptures be fulfilled that describe what must happen now?"

Pointing toward the frenzied mob, Yeshua added, "The cup which my Father has given me, shall I not drink it?"

Peter slunk back into the shadows while Yeshua turned his attention to Malchus, who stood just a few feet away. His face had turned ashen while he held his trembling hand over the raw flesh where his left ear dangled. Blood was squirting between his fingers, sending red rivulets spilling down the side of his face and neck.

Compassion flooded Yeshua's countenance. Taking Malchus by the arm, Yeshua pulled him closer so he could reach out his hand and cover Malchus's bloody one. Yeshua could feel the compassion in his heart overflow until it became virtue pulsating throughout his fingers, sending waves of anointing into the gaping wound on the side of Malchus's head. Yeshua continued to cover the injured area with his hand while his eyes spoke a message of love and forgiveness straight into the soul of his enemy. When Yeshua finally withdrew his hand, the severed ear was positioned perfectly in place, completely healed.

It had all happened so fast that the clamoring mob was unaware of the miracle that had just taken place. But Malchus knew. Withdrawing a few paces from the action, he continued to run his fingers over and over his ear that was now perfectly healed. Yeshua and Malchus locked eyes, and Yeshua knew that Malchus would never be the same. In that instant of time, Malchus had been touched by the power and love of Jehovah. The little insignificant ear wasn't the only thing that had been healed; revelation dawned on the face of the servant of the high priest.

As Yeshua watched transformation take place in Malchus's heart, Yeshua looked beyond the natural realm and saw paraded before his spiritual eyes countless others who century after century would come to the same realization that Malchus had. They too would be made whole—not just in their bodies, but most importantly, their spirits would be made new, and their wounded souls restored.

It will be worth it all, Yeshua thought as he willingly took the first step on the road to man's redemption.

Yeshua moved closer to the soldiers who were holding the chains and held out his hands to be bound. "This is your hour," he said, "and the power which darkness gives you must have its way."

As they led him away into the night, Yeshua could faintly hear fiendish laughter coming from the spirit realm as the minions of darkness gleefully celebrated their first taste of victory.

Chapter Twenty-One

The pesach moon shed a soft glow over the countryside, painting everything in silhouette as the procession of prisoner and captors wound its way from the garden onto the main thoroughfare that led to the city.

As a precaution, the soldiers and the temple guards approached Jerusalem by an indirect route, thinking to avoid contact with the hundreds of pilgrims who had encamped along the western walls of Jerusalem awaiting the Passover (*pesach*) celebration that was to begin at sundown. Marching north until they were past the city, they then dropped down and entered from the west.

The entourage moved on, passing the Antonia fortress manned by Syrian-born soldiers enlisted in Caesar's army. Crossing the viaduct that led to the upper city, the temple guards ushered Yeshua by the light of the full moon out of the fortress area past the Hasmonean palace. Quickly, they proceeded toward a large double courtyard that fronted the Maccabean palace. Thick walls surrounded the palatial homes of Annas and Caiaphas where the grand Sanhedrin was convening to try Yeshua.

As they entered the first courtyard, Annas, a former high priest who now presided over the Sanhedrin, stepped out of the shadows into the center of the courtyard as though he had been waiting for them. Illuminated by several lanterns, he postured himself directly in front of Yeshua and began the inquisition. In an austere manner, Annas questioned Yeshua about his disciples and interrogated him concerning his teaching.

"Nothing I have taught has been spoken secretly. I have spoken openly to the world," Yeshua answered. "Why do you ask me? Ask those who have heard me. They know what I have said."

Without warning, an attendant who was standing next to Annas slapped Yeshua soundly across his mouth. Blood trickled down Yeshua's chin and dripped off his beard.

"How dare you speak to the high priest with disrespect." The portly attendant glared at Yeshua then looked smugly at Annas for approval.

"If I have said anything wrong," Yeshua said as he tried to wipe the blood oozing from the cut on his mouth on the shoulder of his robe. He looked the attendant square in the eyes, "If there was evil in what I said, then tell me what was wrong with it. But if I spoke rightly and properly, why do you strike me?"

Angered at Yeshua's apparent composure, Annas ordered him taken inside to his son-in-law, Caiaphas, where the teachers of the religious law and other leaders had gathered.

A temple guard thrust Yeshua, still bound, through the palace entrance. Dragging him along a marble hallway, the guard shoved him into a huge room filled with religious leaders. There, he was unceremoniously forced to stand before Caiaphas, the ruling high priest.

Inside, confusion reigned. The leading priests and the high council were determined to put Yeshua to death, but to do so, they had to find witnesses to testify against him. The prosecutors had searched and questioned anyone they could find in the dead of night to try to uncover someone who would give evidence. True or false testimonies, they didn't care. They just needed to get a conviction before the Passover officially began the following evening. Every moment was of the essence—never mind that it was illegal to hold a trial at night. This opportunity could not be passed up. Who among the rulers would dare quibble about the fine points of the law?

At last, they found two witnesses who agreed to testify against Yeshua, but they were unable to get their stories together to make a solid case against him.

Frustration set in. Yeshua remained silent, refusing to answer his accusers.

An hour passed, and Caiaphas and the Sanhedrin had made no headway in condemning the prisoner. Annoyed to the depths of his sanctimonious soul, Caiaphas shouted in Yeshua's face, "I demand in the name of the living God that you tell us whether you are the Messiah, the Son of God."

Finally, an accusation Yeshua would be glad to answer. "Yes, it is as you say." Yeshua's face began to radiate with a heavenly glow. "And in the future, you shall see me, the Son of man, sitting on Jehovah's right hand in the place of power and coming back on the clouds of heaven."

Caiaphas jerked back as though he had been slapped. Horrified, he tore his clothing, shouting, "Blasphemy!"

Addressing the crowd of religious leaders, he bellowed, "You have heard his blasphemy. What do you think now?"

A murmur swept through the congregation of religious elites. "He deserves to be put to death." They all agreed as one.

Shouts of "guilty!" filled the early morning air as the religious court pronounced their verdict of death on the Lamb of God.

As the mass of accusers spat in Yeshua's face and slapped and struck him with their fists, at that exact moment across the city in the temple courtyard, one of the priests climbed the temple wall, preparing to signal the start of a new day. He did not know that the day about to begin would divide time for all eternity. It would be a day that would forever separate darkness from light; a day that would never be forgotten throughout ages to come: the Day of Atonement, for all mankind was at long last about to dawn.

Facing east, the priest searched the horizon intently, carefully studying the landscape. Just beyond the city lay the slopes of the Mount of Olives, and across the open fields was the road leading to Bethany. Already, a trickle of faithful Hebrews could be seen making their way toward the Eastern Gate.

For a moment, the priest turned to observe the opposite side of the city. Pilgrims coming up from the Joppa road were also starting to pour in to Jerusalem from the Western Gate. At that moment, the tip of the sun appeared over the eastern hills.

Promptly, temple priests appeared all along the walls of the city raising their horns. In a moment, the air was filled with the loud blast of ram's horns announcing the beginning of the day when thousands of sacrificial lambs would be sacrificed.

It was the first hour of the morning.

While the sunrise began spreading its kaleidoscope of radiance over the horizon and the blast of ram's horns punctuated the stillness of the early morning, the chief priests and the elders of the people held a consultation against Yeshua to put him to death. With their attention focused elsewhere, Yeshua took that opportunity to collapse on a small footstool. Already, he felt drained of strength. The agony in the garden, the walk into the city, and his lack of sleep were taking their toll, and the day had only just begun.

Yeshua knew that the next few hours—his last hours on this earth—were going to be grueling. *Abba Father, strengthen me with might and power within my inner man. Be not far from me, for trouble is near. This is the day that you, O Jehovah, have brought about; I will rejoice and be glad in it.*

No sooner had that silent prayer ascended to the throne of Jehovah than Yeshua felt a change. Life flowed into his every cell as power from on high energized his mortal body. He had no doubt; from that point on, no matter how brutally he would be treated, he could endure.

The next thing Yeshua knew, he was being jerked to his feet once again.

"Take him to the Praetorium," Caiaphas ordered. "He is guilty of blasphemy. This deceiver must be executed."

As they marched back through the streets of Jerusalem toward the palace of Pontius Pilate, multitudes of curiosity seekers began to fall in behind the throng. Even though it was still early, word about Yeshua's conviction and pending sentence spread rapidly throughout the crowd.

"This is the day Pilate releases a prisoner for us in honor of the Passover," a follower of Yeshua pointed out. He leaned closer to his companion. "Don't worry. He will probably release Yeshua."

But Pilate did the unthinkable. Instead of releasing Yeshua, he yielded to the cries of the angry mob that had been whipped into a frenzy by the religious bigots. At the insistence of the throng, Pilate released Barabbas, a notorious prisoner who had been convicted of insurrection and murder.

The decision came as no surprise to Yeshua. *Have I not come to set the prisoners free?* Yeshua felt sorry for the governor. He could see that Pilate had no desire to convict him. In fact, the procurator showed signs of being sympathetic toward his plight.

The dispute went on for some time between Pilate and the religious leaders, but they continued to demand that Yeshua be crucified. Pilate looked as if he were relieved when he discovered that Yeshua was a Galilean, therefore, belonging to Herod's jurisdiction. There was no love lost between him and Herod, and shifting the responsibility for sentencing on Herod pleased him.

When Yeshua was ushered into the king's court, Herod was delighted. He had desired to see the supposed miracle worker for a long time because of what he had heard about him. Herod was hoping to witness some sign or something spectacular. But when Yeshua made no reply to his many questions, his curiosity turned to contempt. Herod and his soldiers commenced to scoff and ridicule him. Finally, dressing him up in bright and gorgeous apparel, King Herod sent Yeshua back to Pilate without a conviction.

Ultimately, when the chief priests and scribes continued to vehemently accuse Yeshua, the procurator eventually gave in. Pilate saw that he was getting nowhere. Afraid that a riot was about to break out, the governor finally took a basin of water and washed his hands in the presence of the crowd.

"I am not guilty of nor bear any responsibility for this righteous man's blood. I find no fault in him. See to it yourselves."

"His blood be on us and on our children. Crucify him!" the people hollered back.

Turning to the soldiers, Pilate said, "Chastise him." He motioned toward the surly mob. "Do as they demand. Crucify him."

As he made the pronouncement of Yeshua's sentence, Pilate looked into Yeshua's eyes, expecting to see fear. Instead, he saw only pity and compassion.

Pilate whirled around and disappeared inside the judgment hall.

The centurion led Yeshua away to the courtyard of the palace where the whole battalion gathered around like an angry pack of hungry wolves. Without delay, the executioners stripped him of his clothes.

Flogging was one sport the cruel and hardened soldiers relished. Two of the most calloused of the regiment picked up a cat of nine tails—a whip with each tail having a piece of metal or bone imbedded in the end of it. Swirling the whips in the air, they practiced their technique by popping their weapons against the pavement a few times, expecting to see the prisoner cringe.

Yeshua didn't move. The explosive sound of metal struck the cobblestones, but Yeshua did not even flinch. In fact, he hardly noticed what was about to happen. His mind was going over and over the prophet Isaiah's messianic prophesy: *But he was wounded for our transgressions, he was bruised for our guilt and iniquities; the chastisement needful to obtain peace and well-being for us was upon him, and with the stripes that wounded him, we are healed and made whole.*

Part of man's redemption was about to take place. Down through the centuries, ever since sin entered the world, Satan had

had the legal right to inflict the bodies of mankind with every kind of sickness and disease imaginable. As long as sin reigned, man was susceptible to the crippling effects of the curse.

Yeshua was aware that because he had never once disobeyed his Father, sin and Satan had no power over his mortal body. The act of yielding his body to be afflicted by the emissaries of hell was the payment needed to obtain healing for Adam's race. The love that pulsated throughout every fiber of Yeshua's being became the armor that would protect his soul. He had come to do the Father's will, and the Father's will was to heal every sickness, disease, and infirmity. This was the price he must pay.

Then the beating began. The soldiers were infuriated at Yeshua's lack of fear. His demeanor was highly unusual. Yeshua's refusal to cower spoiled their sense of power. Determined to break him, the persecutors commenced with savage intensity. Each time the whip struck Yeshua, the tormenter took great pains to drag the lethal instrument across his taut back in a whipping motion, shredding his flesh. The objective was to do the most damage without killing him. Forty lashes would kill. A wrongfully placed lash could disembowel the prisoner. The lashes had to be concentrated on the shoulders, arms, ribs, and down the spinal column. Use of the lash in those areas protected by bone was less likely to kill the prisoner than in the soft flesh of the stomach and kidney area.

Yeshua knew he would not die here. No matter how brutally he was punished, no man, not even Satan himself, could take his life. He would lay down his life at the proper time when redemption was completed, and not before.

The beating went on and on. With every lash, the nerves responsible for sensory perception were exposed, creating pain that was excruciating. Yeshua could feel the horrendous pain. But instead of focusing on the agony, each time he was struck, he pictured those who would believe on him in the years to come— believers who would be redeemed from the sicknesses and infirmities brought on by the curse. As the whip lacerated his flesh, he knew with every stripe healing was being made available to those who were oppressed by Satan.

At last, sickened at the bloody sight, the centurion ordered the soldiers to stop. The human fiends had lacerated Yeshua's body until he was covered with gaping wounds from head to toe. Chunks of flesh were torn from his shoulders, back, and legs where veins had been opened up and nerves exposed. There was hardly a place on his mangled body that was not covered with blood. Red pools gathered on the stones beneath Yeshua's feet as innocent blood poured from the Lamb of God. Yet Yeshua was more conscious of the feeling of love and compassion for his tormentors than the pain that pulsated throughout his body.

Satan's human puppets weren't through yet. They found some thorns about two to three inches long, wood-like and very sharp. Weaving a crown from them, the mockers jammed it on Yeshua's head. To complete the humiliation, they put a reedlike staff in his right hand to represent a scepter. As they beat on the thorns with their staffs, some of the thorns broke off, penetrating Yeshua's skull. This opened up the scalp, causing blood to flow down his face and head. Blood spurted everywhere over Yeshua and his tormentors. That just incited them all the more. Kneeling before him, they made sport of him, chanting, "Hail, King of the Jews."

Then they spat on him. The mockers took turns pulling chunks of beard from his face along with patches of skin. They struck him on the head with a rod. Yeshua spoke not a word nor made an outcry of any sort.

Finally, the soldiers grew weary of the sport. Stripping him of the robe, they put his own garment back on him. As a lamb led to the slaughter and as a sheep before its shearers is dumb, so Yeshua opened not his mouth while the cruel emissaries of darkness led him away to be crucified.

It was the third hour.

Chapter Twenty-Two

The morning sun continued its steady climb toward the apex of the cloudless sky as though this were a day exactly like every other. But invisible beings were aware that this was no ordinary day. Hoards of demonic creatures giddy with maniacal anticipation swarmed around the drama progressing toward the hill just outside the eastern wall of Jerusalem. Hosts of angels stood close by, positioned in a tight battle formation and ready should they be called upon to intervene.

Oblivious to the presence of unseen spectators, the ominous convoy wound its way through the cobblestone streets of lower Jerusalem. Executioners and prisoners, followed by a restless crowd, continued out the eastern Gennath Gate that led to Golgotha—a knoll, which from a distance looked every bit like a bleached skull. Yeshua was the only one in the procession that had any awareness of the magnitude of what was about to take place and how it would affect the world throughout ages to come.

The excruciating pain in his mangled body threatened to drive Yeshua into unconsciousness. Even so, when calloused soldiers had dropped the seventy-five-pound crossbeam across his mutilated shoulders, he had managed to remain upright. Yeshua struggled valiantly to keep up with the rest even though dehydration from loss of blood had drained his physical body of strength. However, when they approached the steep incline that led to the Gennath Gate, he stumbled and lay under the weight of the crossbeam, unable to get up. Even the persistent slicing of the soldier's whips was not enough to force him to his feet.

After a while, the impatient executioners jerked a large man from the crowd, forcing him to bear the weight of Yeshua's burden. Even then, Yeshua had to be half-dragged as he staggered the rest of the distance to the brow of the hill, finally collapsing at the foot of one of three cypress posts anchored in the crown of the skull-like mound.

As Yeshua lay there prostrate, awaiting his execution, he could hear the shrieking cries of the furious mob intermingled with quiet sobs coming from women who were some of his loyal followers.

In the distance, the faint bleating of hundreds of lambs could be heard that were also being carried to their place of death in the temple area. The time for the Passover sacrifice to be offered was fast approaching. Everything was on schedule as it had been determined before the foundation of the earth. Inwardly, Yeshua steeled himself for the final events that would once and for all bring atonement to mankind and seal redemption for the human race.

Barely clinging to life, Yeshua could detect masses of revolting creatures in the spirit realm goading the self-righteous mob until they had become a bloodthirsty den of hate, clamoring for the kill.

They didn't have long to wait. Rome had perfected the art of crucifixion. Adopted from the Phoenicians who preferred a form of execution that was as slow as it was painful, they preferred crucifixion over boiling in oil, stoning, strangulation, impalement, drowning, or burning, which were swifter forms of capital punishment.

"Prepare the prisoners for crucifixion," the centurion barked out to the four soldiers assigned to the task of carrying out the sentences.

Rough hands yanked Yeshua's bloodstained robe and undergarments from his trembling body, leaving him naked and humiliated before the gaping crowd. The next few minutes were a blur of painful torture as his arms were jerked out of socket to line up with the holes already drilled in the cross beam. The cold tips of seven-inch iron spikes pierced his wrists, severing nerves as the nails were pounded in place, sending waves of unimaginable pain through the entire length of his extremities.

To keep from passing out, Yeshua turned his attention from the anguish in his body and focused his mind on the writings of the prophet Isaiah, who hundreds of years before had prophesied about this very moment: "Surely he has borne our diseases, grief, and sicknesses and carried our anguish, affliction, pain, and sorrow, yet we did esteem him stricken, smitten of God and afflicted."

Even though the agony seemed unbearable, Yeshua embraced it willingly. The knowledge that what he was going through was providing deliverance for his beloved creation was enough to remove the horror of the suffering.

Love for all humanity so saturated Yeshua's heart that he hardly felt the full weight of his body being yanked against the spikes impaled in his wrists. The soldiers grasped each side of the crossbeam, lifting it until the mortise fit snugly over the tenon, forming a cross and leaving his feet dangling loosely. From his new vantage point hanging above the crowd, Yeshua allowed his gaze to sweep over the various aspects of people milling below. As the executioner knelt before the cross and positioned Yeshua's right foot on top of the left, driving a third spike through both feet into the hard wood with a measured blow, compassion overwhelmed Yeshua.

Out of the depths of two hearts, Father and Son united as one, came a cry from Yeshua's lips that echoed across Golgotha's plane and down through the years and ages to come. "Father, forgive them, for they do not know what they are doing."

As those words pierced the air, demons from hell fell back in utter confusion. Love had no place in their world, and when it penetrated their realm, upheaval was always the result.

For just a moment below, the executioners and the crowd stood still in bewilderment. The pronouncement they had just heard from the mutilated man hanging before them was highly unusual. Most victims of crucifixion raved like mad men, cursing and screaming obscenities. In extreme cases, soldiers had even been known to cut out a man's tongue to silence him. There was no doubt; this man was different.

As high noon approached, the crowd noticed that something else was different. The light of the sun was beginning to fade, and as the sixth hour drew near, darkness completely covered the whole land.

The darkness that blanketed the earth began to permeate Yeshua's spirit. The hour had come to drink of the cup. In the blackness of that moment, the hand of Elohim appeared before Yeshua bearing a vessel that was so vile and putrid that his righteous soul was repulsed. Everything in him wanted to turn away, but the love that throbbed in his bosom would not allow it. The sins of the whole world—past, present, and future—had been combined into one evil cup, and he who drank of it would become sin personified. Yeshua knew that in the moment he partook of that despicable brew, he would become sin.

Yet Yeshua was willing. He had come from the realm of glory down to a sin-ravaged earth for this very purpose. As Elohim held the cup to Yeshua's trembling lips, he readily allowed the full contents of it to flow into the pit of his being. It was done. There was no turning back. From then on, the court of justice would have its way.

Inside, Yeshua could feel the convulsing effect of sin working death throughout his spirit and soul. The most devastating consequence of sin became evident immediately: separation. The glorious presence of his loving heavenly Father departed, and in its place was a horrifying sense of impending punishment. Guilt, shame, and condemnation washed over Yeshua's soul. He was lost and without Jehovah in this world.

With a loud gut-wrenching cry, Yeshua lifted up his voice. "*Eli, Eli, lama sabachthani?* That haunting question pierced the darkness. "My God, my God, why have you forsaken me?"

For the next hour, Yeshua writhed in pain and torment as his soul agonized and his body fought for breath. His head lolled forward, causing his chin to rest against his chest. His entire weight hung on the spikes in his hands, causing unbearable pain. Cramps knotted the muscles in his arms and shoulders, causing him to twist in agony.

Momentarily, the pectoral muscles at the sides of his chest became paralyzed, making it almost impossible to breathe. Able to inhale but unable to exhale, Yeshua struggled to raise himself up on his wounded feet until finally, his entire weight was supported by the single spike impaled there. With his shoulders level with his hands, he could breathe in ragged gasps. Yeshua fought the ghastly pain in his feet as long as he could, enduring the severe cramps in his legs and thighs in order to breathe for a moment longer. When he could bear the searing pain no longer, he allowed his body to sag against the spikes in his hands once again, and the whole agonizing process began again.

This struggle continued until the ninth hour. Then at last, just as the darkness began to recede and a faint light could be seen, Yeshua pushed up one last time on his throbbing feet and cried out, "It is finished."

Then as he slowly exhaled, Yeshua cried out, "Addoni...into your hands...I commit my spirit."

When he had said that, he breathed his last.

Across the city in the temple courtyard, the mournful blast of a shofar could be heard signaling the beginning of Passover. The hour had come for the sacrifice of the *pesach* lamb. On Golgotha, soldiers pierced the side of the Lamb of God, causing a rush of blood and water to flow down the altar of sacrifice outside the city walls. While inside, the priest sliced the throat of the innocent Passover lamb. Both lambs breathed their last as their blood flowed freely. An innocent life to atone for sin; justice demanded it.

From the holy of holies in heaven, the righteous judge of the universe witnessed the final drop of blood drain from the lifeless body of his only Son. Satisfied, Jehovah made the proclamation that the shed blood was a sufficient atonement for sin.

As that declaration reverberated throughout the heavenly realm, in the holy of holies of the earthly temple where God's presence resided, the sixty-foot-tall and four-inch-thick veil was torn in two from top to bottom. For the first time since sin had entered the world, the way was flung open for each and every person to have free access to Jehovah. The veil that had been a constant reminder of the sin that had caused humanity to be unfit for the presence of Jehovah had been removed. Now a new and glorious way was opened up for Adam's race to approach Elohim with confidence and boldness.

In heaven's eyes, the price had been paid. However, the plan was not complete—not yet. Satan still had to be dealt with. His authority over mankind had to be broken. That battle would take place in the bowels of the earth.

Chapter Twenty-Three

As the last gasping breath escaped from Yeshua's cracked lips, his spirit slipped from his battered body. At that precise moment, the earth beneath began to convulse, heaving and pitching like the sea in the midst of a storm. The onlookers who had remained to watch the crucified victims struggle to live hour after hour screamed in terror. Some beat on their breasts, others ran in fright, but many covered their heads with their cloaks, too panicked to do anything else. Rugged, war-hardened soldiers trembled and fell to their knees.

Amid the chaos, the centurion grasped the foot of the cross, then lifting his eyes to Yeshua's lifeless body, he cried out, "Surely, he was the Son of God!"

The ground beneath Golgotha continued to shake as dark creatures from hell filled the atmosphere like a swarm of blood-sucking insects. To them, the demise of the one called the Word was an unprecedented event to be celebrated. Demons that had grown frustrated following Yeshua around, waiting for an opportunity to spoil his plans, now saw their chance for vengeance.

Angels who had shielded Yeshua from demonic assaults were nowhere to be seen. The glorious covering that had always protected him had been stripped away along with any evidence of the presence of Jehovah. Yeshua seemed to be naked and vulnerable as he entered their realm. The satanic emissaries were jubilant. The Son of God was at their mercy, and they would have no mercy.

Yeshua became aware that he had left his earthly body behind and moved into the domain of the spirit. He was more familiar with that realm than the earthly one, but he had never experienced it like this. Demons were everywhere. They clutched at him with razor-like claws, mauling and yanking him downward.

Directly in front of him, a hole opened on the earth's surface approximately thirty feet in diameter. He could feel a magnetic force sucking him toward the gaping abyss that he had no power to resist. The confidence that been so much a part of him on the earth now had been replaced with a debilitating fear. The sins of the world imbedded in his spirit had changed him from a powerful being into a weak coward.

As he slipped over the edge of the precipice, Yeshua began to plummet down a dark tunnel for what seemed to be miles and miles through darkness that felt as though it had substance, suffocating and distinctively evil. The temperature became unbearably hot the further he descended, sapping every ounce of strength from him.

Finally, after what seemed like hours, Yeshua landed in what appeared to be a huge subterranean cavern. As he looked around, he saw walls that wrapped around on either side covered with hundreds of hideous creatures. Yeshua became aware of a disgusting, putrid stench more revolting than rotten eggs, an open sewer, and rotting flesh all mixed together. The odor itself was enough to cause intense nausea. In the distance, Yeshua could see the flicker of flames from a raging inferno that dimly lit the interior of the cavern.

All at once, Yeshua became conscious of two grotesque beasts that emerged from the darkness on either side. They towered above him some ten to thirteen feet high. Their large, sunken-in eyes, like red, glowing embers, gazed at Yeshua with pure, unrestrained hatred. The giant beings resembled reptiles in human form. One was huge and stout, covered with bumps and scales all over his misshapen body with sharp, gigantic fangs protruding from a huge jaw. The other creature was tall and skinny with long, thin arms; dreadful fins that looked razor-sharp covered his entire body. Sticking out from the ends of his hands were pointed claws nearly twelve inches long. Both glared at Yeshua like he was a fly caught in a web, helpless and trapped.

"Some Son of God you are," snarled the stout one. "You are nothing but a pathetic pile of sinful trash."

Then with strength a thousand times stronger than any man, the beast picked Yeshua up and flung him against the wall of the cave. As he slammed against the side of the cavern, creatures that had been perched against the enclosure scattered like bats frightened out of their niche.

The second creature grabbed Yeshua from behind and sliced open his back with its jagged fins. Then whirling him around like a toy, he thrust his claws into his chest, ripping it open. Yeshua screamed in pain. The anguish he had experienced at the cross was nothing compared to the agony assaulting him here.

Then the area became filled with beings of every despicable shape and size. Some were in the form of gigantic rats and huge spiders at least three feet wide and two feet tall. All sizes of snakes and worms slithered underfoot. Each one was the very epitome of evil. There was no doubt; Yeshua was in hell.

Then the torture began in earnest. Fiendish demons, cauldrons of evil and death, took sadistic pleasure in assaulting Yeshua. The torment continued day and night until the hopelessness and agony became horrendous.

So this is what it feels like to be lost for eternity. The tormentors had let up for an instant, allowing Yeshua time to have a rational thought. As he curled up in a fetal position during the brief period of reprieve, Yeshua could understand why Jehovah didn't want any of his creation to have to experience this horrible place. It had been created for Satan and his angels, but iniquity had created an entrance into this world for transgressors from the human race.

Somewhere in the distance, Yeshua could hear shrieks and moans punctuated by an occasional scream echoing against the cavern walls. The despair and loneliness was an overpowering weight that crushed every portion of his being.

Just when Yeshua felt that he could not stand any more agony, the brutal torture began again. It was not just the physical anguish he had to endure, but the tormentors bombarded him with cruel, mental assaults as well.

"Where is your God now?" they mocked.

"If he loved you, he would never have left you alone."

"You are a nothing; a nobody."

"You will never get out of here. This is your punishment for being such a wicked sinner. This is where you will spend eternity."

"Forever…forever…forever…"

Yeshua clamped his hands over his ears to block out the hideous laughter, but to no avail. The taunts penetrated from every direction.

Then unexpectedly, the atmosphere became deathly still. All activity ceased. An eerie presence pervaded the area.

Yeshua's eyes darted around furtively. Then abruptly out of the murky shadows, a form began to materialize in the center of the grotto. The creature that took shape was clothed in gaudy attire that seemed to fill the region with a sinister pageantry. Yeshua had no doubt who stood before him: the fallen archangel, Satan himself, nemesis to Jehovah and the human race.

Instead of the beautiful being that Yeshua had faced in the wilderness, now Satan's countenance was twisted into a grotesque mask with black strands of oily hair plastered close to his head. His fingers, long and bony, were shaped like claws, and his teeth hung like tarnished daggers from a gaping mouth frozen into an evil smirk.

"So we meet once again, loser." Satan thrust a twisted wand in Yeshua's direction. "Bring him to me," he ordered.

The beast standing closest to Yeshua seized him by the hair and hurled him through the air. Yeshua crumbled in a heap at Satan's feet. Satan howled in fiendish glee.

"Not so high and mighty now, I see." Satan kicked Yeshua in the face with a hoofed foot. "Defeat me? Never! Not a useless piece of flesh like you."

Whirling around in a wild, erratic motion, he lifted both hands in the air. And then throwing back his head, Satan let out a shriek of triumph that rattled the corridors of hell.

"Going to crush my head, were you? I don't think so. You are mine, and I will do with you as I please for as long as I wish, and there is nothing you can do to stop me."

Yeshua struggled to rise on one knee, but Satan shoved him back down with a quick blow. Then placing one foot on Yeshua's head, he crowed, "Now who is going to crush whose head?"

Satan's maniacal laughter echoed throughout the cavern as demons from the farthest boundaries of Hades joined in with their heinous refrain.

Suddenly, Satan stopped and jerked Yeshua to his feet. Leering in his face, Satan waved a boiling, frothing cup of iniquity and death in Yeshua's face. "This, my pathetic opponent, gives me the legal right to rule over planet earth, and now nothing can stop me from dominating the universe. Your plan has failed. Since you have drunk from this cup, you too, Jehovah's precious son, have become just like the others: a sinner under the sentence of death and subject to my authority."

Once again, coarse laughter filled the atmosphere. Satan and his demons were so busy celebrating they failed to notice that a change was beginning to take place in Yeshua.

Yeshua became aware of a shaft of light that penetrated the dense darkness of hell. More importantly, Yeshua detected something happening inside his heart. Before, it had been squeezed and twisted with shame and condemnation, but now, at last, the massive burden of oppression was being lifted from him.

Strength flowed once again into his inner being as Yeshua experienced, right there in the pit of hell, cleansing from the dreadful effects of sin. Then he heard the voice of his Father whisper in his ear, "Though your sins be as scarlet, they shall be as white as snow; though they be red like crimson, they shall be as wool."

It all came back to him in a burst of revelation: the sacrificial lamb that shed its innocent blood, and the scapegoat, the goat that carried the sins of the people into the wilderness, that was why he was in this horrible place. He had borne the iniquity of Adam's race into the bowels of the earth where it had originated. Since one man's trespass had unleashed Satan's authority into the earth, now, through one man—his obedience to become the sacrificial lamb—he had won it back. Yeshua was overjoyed. *The scarlet cloth attached to the scapegoat had turned white.* Justice required that the penalty for sin be paid only one time, not over and over as it had been in the past. The total payment for all sin had now been completed.

After a moment, Satan once again whirled back around toward Yeshua, intending to gloat, expecting to find him still cowering at his feet. But instead of reveling in triumph, Satan began to tremble when he caught sight of Yeshua's face. Something wasn't right. Yeshua stood before him poised and confident with no sign of the abuse he had undergone. The white, glistening robe that clothed him was so brilliant that Satan had to turn his head away because of the pain caused by the intense light. In Yeshua's hand, he held a beautiful scepter made of gold and crowned with sparkling jewels.

"What...what...is happening?" As Satan started to stumble backward, he glanced at the contents of the cup he was still holding. He screamed in horror at what he saw and hurled it to the floor. Instead of the evil brew of death and iniquity that had been there only moments before, now flowing from its depths was a fountain of blood—the blood of the Lamb.

Yeshua bent over and picked up the cup. Holding it up in triumph, Yeshua's eyes flashed with righteous fire as he fixed his eyes squarely on Satan. "I now hold the keys to death and hell."

Waving the blood-filled vessel in Satan's ashen face, he announced, "I declare, from now on and for as long as time exists, anyone who believes in me will be cleansed from his sins and henceforth receive the gift of righteousness."

Then Satan recoiled as Yeshua's voice thundered throughout Hades, reaching into the entire spirit realm. Like the sound of a trumpet, Yeshua heralded the transfer of earth's authority as he notified Satan with great delight, "Those who have been redeemed by the blood of the Lamb shall reign over your kingdom forevermore."

As those words pierced the darkness, the power of the Holy Spirit exploded into the pit of hell. Satan and every demon fell prostrate on the cavern floor as though dead.

For just one moment, Yeshua placed his foot soundly on the serpent's head and then steadily began to ascend up the tunnel. Where three days before he had descended a filthy sinner impregnated with the sins of the world, now he ascended, a righteous man cleansed by the blood of the Lamb, raised to new life—the firstborn of a new creation.

Chapter Twenty-Four

The sun released its multicolored glow on the eastern horizon framing the Mount of Olives with a brilliance that tinted the dawn with the promise of a new beginning. It was the start of a new week and a new day for mankind. Nature seemed to know it was a day of celebration. Birds flitted in and out of the branches of the olive trees chirping their melodious praises to their Creator. A crisp, gentle breeze caused the trees and shrubberies to sway in harmony as though they were clapping their hands in rhythm to an invisible orchestra.

The radiance of the morning was in stark contrast to the pall of oppression that had blanketed Jerusalem for the past three days. Passover activities had proceeded as usual, but a shadow of melancholy permeated the mood of the pilgrims as the silhouettes of three crosses leered at them from Golgotha. News had spread rapidly about the crucifixion of Yeshua. Many who less than a week before had passionately cheered in admiration were now mourning. They had been convinced that Yeshua was the promised Messiah, but now their hopes had been dashed. He was dead.

In the heart of Jerusalem, disciples who had gathered early that morning sat huddled in the upper guest chamber of the same house where only days before they had shared a supper with their beloved Master. They had not known at the time that they were eating the last supper they would ever eat with him. Fear gripped them. But more than that, they were ashamed and devastated. Various emotions tore their insides apart. Nearly every one of them had deserted their teacher and mentor in the very hour he had needed them most. They had wept until they had no more tears to shed.

For Peter, the agony was intensified. Not only had he deserted his friend, he had vigorously denied that he even knew him. He was a coward, and he knew it. Bitter tears had not erased the humiliation of what he had done. The other disciples seemed to understand why he had done what he did—after all, they had practically done the same themselves—but he would never have a chance to tell Yeshua he was sorry. That part was eating away at him.

They sat in silence, too distraught to make conversation. For the last three days, they had gone from house to house where they had lodged with various followers during the Passover festivities. They discussed over and over again every detail of the horrifying events, but now, they had nothing left to say. The one who had been the Messiah in their eyes was nothing more than a miracle-working prophet who would pass into the pages of history—someone who had changed some lives temporarily. But now, life would go on as usual. Tyranny would prevail; twisted, crippled humanity would remain the same; and hope would waste away. Even as dawn penetrated the horizon, darkness was suffocating the hearts of the disciples.

Abruptly, the men were brought out of their stupor by a frantic pounding at the door. No one moved. They had not shown their faces in public since the crucifixion even though they had felt fairly safe because of the Passover Sabbath. Members of the Sanhedrin would do nothing during the high feast days. However, the Sabbath was over, and who knew what they would be facing in the days to come. Yeshua had said they would be persecuted for their loyalty to him, but now he was gone. Surely the religious leaders would leave them alone. Nevertheless, they had gone into hiding just in case.

The pounding continued. Still, no one made a sound. Fear was a tangible presence that seemed to have a paralyzing effect. After a few more seconds, they heard a muffled voice shouting, "Peter, John, are you in there?"

When Peter recognized the voice of Mary Magdalene, he hurried to the door. Mary almost fell into the room as Peter flung it open.

Regaining her footing, she gasped for breath. "He…he isn't there…he's gone…" She paused to catch her breath.

"What are you talking about?" Peter grabbed Mary by the shoulders. "What do you mean he's gone? Who's gone?" The other disciples pressed in closer.

Finally, Mary was able to slow down a bit, but her distress was unmistakable. "Yeshua! His body is not there. We…me and some other women went to the tomb a little while ago…the stone was rolled away, and the guards were gone. Didn't you feel the earthquake?"

The disciples all shook their heads. "Anyway," Mary continued, "when we got there, and we couldn't figure out how we were going to roll the stone away, but it was already rolled away. I already said that, didn't I?"

Mary took another deep breath while she brushed a strand of hair out of her eyes. Peter was growing impatient. "What are you trying to tell us?"

"I'm saying that Yeshua's body is not there. Someone has taken him away." Mary began to sob. "I-I don't know where they've taken him." She sniffed and wiped her hand across her eyes. "Do you know where he is?"

"What?" Peter looked at the other disciples with an incredulous expression. "Are you saying his body is gone?"

Mary nodded through her tears. However, before she could say another word, Peter charged out the door with John at his heels. Mary trailed along as fast as she could, but they easily outran her.

It took only a few minutes for the men to race the distance to the gravesite. When Peter and John arrived puffing and panting, they could see that it was just like Mary had said. The stone was positioned on one side of the entrance, and the guards were nowhere to be seen. John tried to catch his breath before entering, but as he peered inside, he could just make out in the murky shadows a pile of linen cloths on the ledge where the body was supposed to be.

Peter didn't waste any time stopping. He rushed on in. There, he also saw the linens. But what drew his attention was the burial napkin that had been wound around Yeshua's head still rolled up, lying in a place by itself.

It just didn't make sense. Peter became aware that John had entered the tomb and was now standing by his side. John noticed the burial napkin too. He whispered in awe, "It's just like he said. He's alive." John grabbed Peter in a bear hug. His voice rose in excitement. "He has risen. Yeshua is alive!"

Peter drew back from John's embrace with a puzzled expression. "No, we don't know that for sure." He shook his head. "There could be any number of explanations."

By that time, Mary had joined them and added her theory about what had happened. After several minutes of heated discussion, Peter and John headed back to the house, but Mary decided to stay by the tomb. She reasoned that maybe whoever had taken the body would return, and she wanted to be there.

All the way back to their lodging, Peter and John argued back and forth. John's belief could not be shaken. He was convinced what they had seen was signs of a resurrection. No matter how Peter tried to come up with a logical explanation, John stuck by his convictions.

As Peter and John approached the dwelling where several of the disciples remained, Peter hesitated. Then placing his hand on John's arm, he said, "I don't feel much like going inside."

He pointed toward the stairway that led to the upper chamber. "You, go on up and tell the others what we have found. I-I need some time to think this through."

Shaking his head, he turned to go. His shoulders slumped as though carrying a heavy, invisible load; his chin rested against his chest. He stumbled through the network of streets that wound through the interior of lower Jerusalem until he arrived at the house where he had been lodging. It was still early enough in the morning that only a few vendors were out heading for their places of business. Occasionally, the clip clop of donkeys' hooves broke the stillness along with the whinny of a stabled horse impatiently waiting for its morning feeding.

Instead of going inside, Peter found a secluded area in the back where he dropped to the ground and leaned back against a tall sycamore tree. A gentle breeze stirred the branches overhead while the trill of a mocking bird serenaded the morning. But the only mocking Peter noticed was what was going on in his mind; it was whirling in turmoil. A variety of emotions churned inside, tumbling over each other and causing his head to pound. Guilt and regret hammered away at his heart as he recounted over and over again what he had done. The scene played itself out in his mind's eye: the courtyard…the accusations…his denial… the cock crowing…and finally the sorrow in Yeshua's eyes as he passed through the courtyard…

How could I have been so weak? Peter dropped his head into his hands. Rocking back and forth, he clutched fistfuls of hair. *What if Yeshua is alive again? How could I ever face him, and what would he do to me?* Tears coursed down Peter's weathered cheeks, disappearing into his bushy beard. Despair pressed so heavily upon his heart that he felt it would burst into pieces from the weight.

Several minutes passed as Peter continued to agonize. But then, all at once, he became aware of someone standing directly in front of him. When he lifted his eyes to observe the intruder, Peter jumped to his feet and staggered backward.

"Yeshua, Yeshua, is-is that you?" Peter grasped his hands over his throat.

"Yes, Peter," Yeshua answered gently. "I have arisen as I said I would."

Peter stood staring at the man he had spent hundreds of hours following around the country. He had watched him perform miracle after miracle and had listened as he had taught and preached about every aspect of the kingdom of heaven, but in the end, he had denied that he knew him. Remorse like a burdensome cross dug its weight into his shoulders.

Peter could bear the pain no longer. As Yeshua held out his hands to Peter, he collapsed prostrate at Yeshua's feet. When he noticed the gaping holes, evidence of where a spike had been driven, Peter laid his forehead against the wounds and wept.

Through heart-wrenching sobs, Peter cried, "Master, can-can you ever forgive me for what I have done?" His large shoulders shook as he bathed Yeshua's feet with his tears.

Yeshua bent over and rested his nail-scarred hands on Peter's shoulders. In a tender voice, he said, "Arise."

As Peter struggled to stand up, Yeshua cupped his hands on either side of Peter's rugged, tear-stained face. Peter found himself looking into eyes that seemed to be liquid pools of love—love so complete that it overflowed into rivers of forgiveness.

"Yes, Peter, you are forgiven. Do you not remember that I told you what would happen beforehand, and that I had already prayed for you? My son, don't allow your faith to fail."

Peter felt the strength of Yeshua's arms as he drew him to his breast in a warm embrace. For a moment, Peter allowed his head to rest on Yeshua's shoulder as the weight of condemnation gave way to a flood of peace that rushed throughout the depths of his being.

Yeshua drew back and once again looked directly into Peter's eyes. With a smile that seemed to rival the brilliance of the morning sun, Yeshua said, "Now, Peter, go and strengthen your brethren."

Peter turned momentarily to look in the direction Yeshua was pointing, but when Peter turned back around, Yeshua was no longer there. He had vanished as though he had disappeared into the air. But the joy that filled Peter's heart was still there.

Peter's feet felt as light as his heart. He wasted no time as he raced through the cobbled streets to the house where the disciples had gathered. Charging up the steps, he burst through the door. "He's alive!" he fairly shouted.

The room was packed with disciples and followers who had assembled from various parts of the city as news of Yeshua's missing body had circulated. Mary, who had been the center of attention until Peter arrived, rushed to Peter's side. He grabbed her in a fierce hug and spun her around. "He's alive, he's really alive. I've just seen him."

"I know." Mary shook her head vigorously when Peter finally set her down. "I've seen him too." She gestured wildly. "I was standing by the tomb after you left…I saw an angel…was he ever glorious…he talked to me…and then…" Mary caught her breath as her face lit up with a glow that told the rest of the story better than any words could describe.

"Then I saw him," she whispered in awe. "I didn't know him at first, but then he spoke my name. There's no one who says it like he does, and I knew him."

The other disciples moved in closer to Peter and Mary. Eagerly, they listened as Peter described in its entirety his encounter with the Master. Hours passed as they discussed in animated terms what it all meant. As more of Yeshua's followers joined the already crowded room, someone brought out some bread and fish along with a bowl of figs and a cluster of grapes. Although most had not eaten all day, no one really cared. As the evening shadows lengthened outside and the sun began to dip behind the horizon, the group finally decided to eat something before they dispersed for the night.

Just as Peter had finished blessing the bread, they heard a frantic banging on the door. Seconds later, Cleopas and Lucius hurriedly entered, puffing and panting as though they had run a long distance without stopping. When they were finally able to speak, they reported in lively detail the extraordinary experience that had occurred while they had been traveling along the road to Emmaus.

They told how a stranger had joined them, and how they had discussed the happenings concerning Yeshua's crucifixion. They shared with the disciples how their hearts had fairly burned within them as the man, line upon line, had made clear the reason Messiah had to suffer before entering into his glory. Then beginning with Moses and the prophets, the traveler had explained and interpreted the Scriptures concerning the Messiah.

"When we arrived at Emmaus, we invited him in to eat and lodge with us for the night," Cleopas said. "As we reclined at the table, he took the bread and gave thanks. But it was when he spoke the blessing and broke the bread that we knew." Cleopas looked knowingly at Lucius.

"It was as though our eyes were instantly opened," Lucius added. "And we recognized him." With tears in his eyes, Lucius's gaze swept over the group who were eagerly hanging on their every word. "It was him," he said in awe. "Yeshua himself."

"He is alive," Cleopas added in a hushed tone.

A low murmur swept through the assembly. First Mary, then Peter, now these two—the truth was beginning to sink in. Was it possible that Yeshua was really alive and that he had indeed risen?

As they continued to discuss the extraordinary turn of events, suddenly, a light flashed throughout the room with pulsating intensity, and in its midst stood Yeshua. They recognized him, but his apparel and his countenance radiated a brightness that was not of this world. Most of the disciples were so startled and shocked that many thought they were seeing a ghost. Trembling, some fell on their knees in fright while others clung to one another for support. But Peter and Mary knew. This was not a ghost; the one that stood before them was their Messiah—the risen Lord.

The fear that had gripped the other disciples turned to joy as they heard the voice of their beloved teacher once again. "Why are you disturbed and troubled?" Yeshua asked. "And why do questions arise in your hearts?"

He held out his hands so everyone could see the holes that penetrated both of his wrists. Then lifting his robe, the wounds on his feet came in to view. "See my hands and feet." Stretching out his arm toward Matthew, he said, "Feel me and see. A spirit does not have flesh and bones as you see that I have."

Then to prove once and for all that they were not just seeing a spirit or a vision, he asked for something to eat. After eating a piece of boiled fish that Thaddeus grabbed from a dish on the table, Yeshua said to them, "This is what I told you while I was still with you. Everything that is written concerning me in the Law of Moses, the prophets, and also the Psalms had to be fulfilled."

Then gazing around the room at his loyal followers, Yeshua continued, "It was written that the Messiah would suffer and on the third day rise from the dead so that forgiveness of sins could be preached in his name to all nations—beginning right here in Jerusalem. Now you are witnesses that these things have certainly come to pass."

Extending both hands toward the group who seemed to be frozen in place, Yeshua looked from one to the other until he had acknowledged every one. "As the Father has sent me forth, so I am sending you."

Having said this, he breathed on them and said, "Receive the Holy Spirit."

In that moment, each one felt as though an invisible hand reached down into their sin-laden hearts, removing the contamination caused by the iniquities of the past. And in its place a brand-new heart was inserted, cleansed, and purified.

Those in the room couldn't contain their joy. Peter and John hugged each other; Mary danced while others shouted praises to

Jehovah in uninhibited ecstasy. Their sins had been forgiven, and they knew it. It felt as if their old lives had passed away, and they had become new creatures.

The room was filled with such exuberances that they were unaware when Yeshua disappeared from their midst as though he had just walked through the closed door without opening it. Even though he had vanished, they could still feel his presence inside their hearts.

Word of what had happened spread rapidly throughout Jerusalem. During the next few weeks, they and numerous others had similar experiences, not just in Jerusalem, but also around Galilee where the angels had told Mary that Yeshua would meet his disciples.

• • • • • • • • • • • • • • • • • •

Forty days had passed since Yeshua's first appearance to the disciples on that unforgettable resurrection day. Much had changed in their lives. During that time, they had begun to understand more clearly aspects of the kingdom of God from conversations they had had with Yeshua at various times.

They had almost grown accustomed to Yeshua showing up unexpectedly from time to time. Excitement had begun to stir throughout their company. Was it possible that this would be the time he would restore Israel back to its former glory and bring deliverance from Rome's tyranny?

One day as they were gathered together back in Jerusalem discussing these possibilities, Yeshua appeared in the room where they were reclining at the table. Although the disciples were not as startled at Yeshua's visitations as they had been right after his resurrection, still they were amazed and in awe of his presence every time he appeared.

As Yeshua stood before them radiant with the vitality of heaven, a hush filled the room along with a sense of reverence that left the men speechless. Finally, Phillip broke the silence.

Considering what they had been talking about before the Master appeared, he asked, "Lord, is this the time when you will reestablish the kingdom and restore it to Israel?"

Yeshua shook his head as he positioned himself at the table with them. "It is not for you to know the time or seasons that the Father has chosen."

Then resting both hands on the table, he leaned toward them, letting them know that the restoration of Israel was not what was foremost on his mind, but rather the restoration of mankind. He said earnestly, "But you shall receive power after the Holy Spirit has come upon you, and you shall be my witnesses in Jerusalem and all Judea and Samaria and to the ends of the earth."

He let that sink in for a moment then added, "Go into the entire world and preach the good news of the gospel to the whole human race. Everyone who believes and is baptized will be saved from the penalty of eternal death, but he who does not believe will be condemned."

Yeshua continued to instruct the men while they ate. When they finished, Yeshua arose. Usually, he would just disappear, but the disciples were surprised when Yeshua motioned for them to follow him as he headed for the door. They glanced at each other with questions in their eyes. Something was different about this appearance. They had a feeling that something unusual was about to happen.

It seemed like old times as they followed him down the familiar route through the streets of Jerusalem and out the Western Gate that led to the Mount of Olives where the disciples had spent many long hours with Yeshua.

Although Yeshua walked along at a leisurely pace, his stride was purposeful as though on a mission. He appeared to be in deep thought and said nothing as they ascended the incline up the side of the mount. As they reached the summit of the hill where Yeshua had preached some of his greatest sermons, his followers gathered around.

Yeshua faced them with the fire of triumph in his eyes. "All authority and all power to rule in heaven and on earth have been given to me," he said.

The force of that pronouncement hit the disciples with an impact that felt almost tangible. Then he stopped and opened his pierced hands before them. "Now, I give to you the keys of the kingdom. You go in my name and in my authority. These signs will accompany anyone who believes in my name: they will drive out demons; they will speak with new tongues; they will pick up serpents; and even if they drink anything deadly, it will not hurt them; they will lay their hands on the sick, and the sick will be healed."

For the next several minutes, Yeshua passionately described what had happened in the bowels of the earth and how Satan had been stripped of his authority. He explained that because of his victory over Satan, anyone, henceforth, who believed on him would have power over the devil and his kingdom. Yeshua made clear that whatever they bound on earth was what would be bound in the heavenlies, and whatever they loosed on earth in his name would be carried out in the spirit realm.

"I want you to know," he said, "the One that is in you is greater than the power of the evil one."

Yeshua allowed his gaze to rest, one by one, on the men who had loved and stuck by his side through the joys and sorrows of the past three and a half years. A tender expression enveloped his countenance as he stretched out his hands and began to pray a blessing over them.

Lifting up his eyes, he prayed, "Jehovah, my Father, these men have done me honor, and my glory has been achieved in them."

Upon hearing those words, Peter and the rest of the men felt a deep sense of gratitude well up inside at the complete forgiveness that had been granted to them. They certainly had not honored or glorified Yeshua only a few weeks before. They blinked as moisture filled their eyes.

Yeshua continued, "Keep them in your name that they may be one as we are one that the world may know that you sent me and that you have loved them even as you have loved me."

A heavenly glow radiated from Yeshua's face. "I do not ask that you take these out of the world, but that you keep and protect them from the evil one."

By then, the disciples could almost feel the holy presence of heavenly beings positioned all around. As they looked into the face of their risen Lord, the love that emanated from his countenance penetrated the deepest recesses of their souls, filling them with undeniable joy and perfect peace.

Yeshua continued, "Sanctify them and make them holy by the truth; your Word is truth. Just as you sent me into this world, now I also send them into the world. Neither do I pray for these alone, but also for all those who will come to believe in me through their words and teachings in centuries to come."

Tears coursed unchecked down the disciple's faces as Yeshua's words washed over them, bathing them with a powerful sense of destiny.

"Father, I desire that all of those whom you have entrusted to me may be with me where I am, so that they may see my glory which you have given me."

A holy hush settled on the hilltop as a cloud slowly descended. Yeshua drew the prayer to a close. "And now I am coming to you, my Addoni; may the love that you have bestowed upon me be felt in the hearts of those who believe on me and that I may be in them."

When he had finished, Yeshua lifted his hands in a benediction as the cloud enveloped him. Steadily, Yeshua began to rise as he ascended heavenward out of the disciples' sight.

Then, while the disciples stood motionless, gazing intently toward heaven where Yeshua had disappeared, two men dressed in glistening robes suddenly stood beside them.

"Men of Galilee, why do you stand gazing into heaven?" one of the angels asked. "This same Yeshua who has been caught away will return in just the same way in which you saw him go into heaven."

So a new race was birthed upon the earth. Men and women who were born again and transferred from the kingdom of darkness into the kingdom of Jehovah's dear Son—a new creation over which the god of the world had no power—ones who were commissioned to storm the gates of hell, to tear down the strongholds of evil, and destroy the ravages of sickness and disease. Believers, clothed in robes of righteousness who had the power to rule and reign in the world through the blood of the Lamb—forgiven.

Chapter Twenty-Five

Satan watched in relief as Yeshua ascended through the second heaven and on into the third heaven. Good riddance. That's where he needed to be. Out of his sight forever, he hoped. Yeshua had wrecked enough havoc in his kingdom, stripping him of his coveted authority right there in his own territory. Satan was livid. At least he wouldn't have to contend with Yeshua any longer. He had left the earth and the authority in the hands of a few puny disciples. How could a small number of uneducated peasants do any harm to his realm? Satan prepared to operate as usual.

However, Satan's relief turned to near panic when ten days later outer space was split with a roar like the sound of a rushing, mighty wind. Something was coming down from heaven. Demons quaked in fear. Satan watched in horror as the Holy Spirit filled one hundred and twenty of Yeshua's followers in an upper room right there in the heart of Jerusalem. Satan wasn't sure what that would mean for him, but he knew it couldn't be good.

Sure enough, those few devotees began to act just like Yeshua acted when he had been on the earth. Now Satan and his demons didn't have just one powerful opponent to deal with. Before the day was over, those one hundred and twenty had turned into three thousand. A few days later five thousand more sprung up. Every day, more and more believers were added to the opposition force. Like ants, they scurried everywhere, and everywhere they went, it was as if the world was turned upside down, especially Satan's world. Miracles, signs and wonders, and sick folks getting healed by just coming in contact with the shadow of one of those spirit-filled creatures; it was enough to turn the stomach of any devil.

Something had to be done, or this would get totally out of hand. His kingdom was being demolished, and his whole hierarchy thrust into confusion. The first thing that came to mind was death. If there are pests bothering you, what do you do? You kill them, of course. Finding somebody to handle that job would be easy. There was always someone or a whole group of humans who could be manipulated to become his executioners.

So the killing began. Satan chose those he had used before as his puppets to do the job. Why mess with success? The religious hierarchy was easy. They were so full of pride that anything taught against their doctrine was worthy of death. Hadn't they proved that when they crucified Yeshua?

The persecution grew in intensity. Satan had selected an especially arrogant Pharisee named Saul of Tarsus. He was zealous. Satan liked that. Saul was wild, devastating the church with cruelty and violence, entering house after house, and dragging men and women off to jail.

But that tactic seemed to backfire. The persecution simply scattered the fanatics throughout the land where they continued to spread their damnable doctrine of salvation. Instead of exterminating the pests, they just grew in number. A huge blow struck at the heart of Satan's scheme when his chief henchman turned traitor. It was unbelievable. After a couple of years of undisputed success, Saul became a follower of Yeshua. What was going on was more powerful than anything Satan had ever encountered before.

Years passed, and Satan was no closer to stamping out the dreaded invasion by the radicals who called themselves Christians than when he started. In fact, they were multiplying faster than he could keep track of. So he turned up the intensity of persecution to include torture. He enlisted the services of the Roman authorities—even Caesar himself. Christians were thrown to lions, tortured, cut in two, burned alive—still, their numbers grew.

Finally, Satan decided to rethink his strategy. If he had known all this was going to happen, he would not have crucified Yeshua. With all those humans endued with the authority he once had, he was finding it more and more difficult to get any momentum going. Just when he thought he was gaining ground, someone would come against him in *that name,* and his progress would be bound, and his demons cast out. He had to stand by helpless while the work of Jehovah continued unhindered. It was maddening.

Suddenly, a thought came to him: *What if those so-called Christians didn't realize they have authority over my kingdom? Just suppose they believed that what I am doing is really the will of God. Of course, that's it. Why haven't I thought of that before? Then they wouldn't resist me, and I would have free reign over the earth.*

Satan still had one powerful weapon that couldn't be taken from him. He might not have undisputed authority anymore, but he could lie, seduce, and deceive to perfection. His favorite tool was to sabotage Jehovah's reputation. Confuse the issue. Make Jehovah out to be part good and part evil. The plan was ingenious. Yes, it would work. But first, he had to get rid of the truth. A lie would always be in jeopardy when truth was readily available.

So it began with incarcerating the Word of God in institutions of higher spiritual learning available to just a few selected folks. The dark ages of history had begun. As Satan twisted what truth they knew, lies and deception began to spread like a cancer throughout the Christian world. Miracles ceased, sickness and diseases were attributed to Jehovah's will, and mayhem and war came with the approval of Jehovah because, after all, they reasoned, God was in charge; therefore, no matter what happened, he must have allowed it. Little did the Christians know that with the authority of heaven and the Holy Spirit to guide them, they were in charge. Satan chuckled at the irony.

Centuries passed. Only a few throughout the years were able to uncover snippets of truth. Certainly, there were always many in every generation that escaped Satan's grasp and became followers of Yeshua—more than Satan would like to admit—but their power was limited unless somehow they happened to uncover the truth about the mighty power that was within them and the authority Yeshua had invested in them. A few did, but only a few. If Satan had his way, the majority would never find out.

Nineteen hundred years had gone by, and the world had experienced suffering, disease, calamity, and tragedy at the hand of Satan without many repercussions from the kingdom of light. He had struck a huge blow to the European population by killing seventy-five million people with the Black Death in the mid-1300s. He saw to it that over the three centuries between the 1600s and the 1800s, continents were scourged by deadly epidemics such as Cholera, Small Pox, and Yellow Fever. When he threw a few wars and crusades in the mix, Satan could see that his plan was working satisfactorily and his kingdom was intact—that is until the turn of the nineteenth century.

Satan's habit of releasing plagues on the earth was one of his greatest delights. They were his masterpieces. A well-placed plague could destroy thousands or even millions without much effort on his part. The bubonic plague was especially hideous, resplendent with grotesque suffering. He had used it quite effectively in the thirteenth and fourteenth centuries, so well in fact that this was his favorite means of inflicting anguish on the human race. As the twentieth century began, Satan commanded his special forces of darkness—spirits of infirmity—to infest a particular area in Australia with the plague's infection. Not long thereafter, the scourge began to spread throughout the land. Satan sat back preparing to enjoy the action. His hideous laughter rocked the second heaven. Nothing could stop him now—or so he thought.

Chapter Twenty-Six

Sydney, Australia, 1901

As a new day peeked over the horizon, rays of sunlight struggled to lighten the gray dawn amid the relentless rain that had started pounding away once again at the window pane of John's study. John's eyes snapped open. *Where am I?*

He could feel the hard leather crease pressing into his back that had always made the lounge so uncomfortable. He had fallen asleep sometime in the night. About midnight, his eyes had gotten so heavy he had decided to take just a short lie down. The last thing he remembered was stretching out and propping his feet up on the arm of the lounge.

He glanced at the clock. Five o'clock. He had slept for at least five hours. His eyes felt like sandpaper from all the tears he had shed the day before and the hours of reading afterward. As he pulled his protesting body to a sitting position, memories of the events from the day before brought back the agonizing grief that had been briefly blocked out by slumber. Sarah was dead, along with thirty-one faithful members of his church, and who knew how many more would die before it was all over? For hours, John had searched his Bible for answers—anything that would shed light on why a loving God would allow such suffering. He buried his face in his hands for a moment to massage the dull ache behind his eyes.

Yesterday afternoon, John had secluded himself in his study for one reason and one reason only: he had been desperate for answers—answers that could come only from God; man had no remedy. Hour after hour, he had explored the pages of the Bible as though he were digging for hidden treasure. He had read about the fall of man, the life and ministry of Jesus—the miracles, signs and wonders, and healing of the multitudes—and finally his death, resurrection, and ascension. He had read the many stories that had become so familiar to him over the years. They had inspired him just as they always had—especially the accounts of Jesus healing the sick. But where was that healing Jesus today? That's what he had to find out.

It would be at least a couple of hours before Jeanne would call him for breakfast, so once again he sat down at his desk. In desperation, he picked up his Bible and as he hugged it to his chest, he turned his eyes upward.

"Your message to me, Lord, has to be in this book. Show me your will, O God of truth."

Dropping his head in his hands, he cried out once again, "Jesus, you are the same today as you were back then. Why are the sick not healed? Is this horrible disease really your will?"

Heaven was silent. Not even the whisper of a still, small voice stirred inside. John was about ready to admit defeat when he laid his Bible on the desk and thumbed through its pages one last time. Then, as though an unseen hand reached down and stayed his search, there, laying open in front of him was the tenth chapter of Acts. He felt compelled to focus on that particular passage of scripture. Then as though the brilliance of the noonday sun had condensed into one powerful beam, Acts 10:38 stood out, surrounded with radiant light.

> How God anointed Jesus of Nazareth with the Holy Ghost and with power: who went about doing good, and healing all that were oppressed of the devil; for God was with him.

Understanding was like the suddenness of the flash of a lightning strike. John's eyes were flooded with light—not his physical eyes, but spiritual ones enlightened with faith.

Satan was the defiler, and Christ was the healer. It was as simple as that. He needed no theologian to clarify the issue. The religious experts of his day had only muddied the waters so the real truth had been buried under mountains of church theology gathered from man's reasoning.

That dreadful disease is the foul offspring of its father, Satan, and its mother sin. John thought as he jumped to his feet. The tears were gone. A song of triumph and thanksgiving bubbled up from a heart reinvigorated by faith.

"Jesus, you truly are still the same today as you were when you walked the earth. You, my Savior, still deliver your children from Satan's oppression. It is you who heals, and Satan our adversary who makes sick."

John could hardly contain his excitement.

His moment of revelation was interrupted by the sound of someone banging at the entrance of the parsonage.

Two panting messengers stood at his door, dripping wet. "Pastor, Pastor, come at once! Mary is dying. Come and pray."

John felt like a shepherd that had just heard that one of his prize sheep was being torn from the fold by a cruel wolf. He rushed from his house, snatching an umbrella on his way out. Racing down the street through the rain, he hastened into the room of the dying maiden.

In an instant, he took in the scene that lay before him. The room was sparsely furnished with just a nightstand on which sat a pitcher of water—half empty—and a basin surrounded with several soiled towels. Other rags were draped across the backs of chairs and scattered haphazardly around on the floor. The room smelled of vomit and other disgusting excrement.

Pacing up and down the room was Dr. Worthington, a good Christian man whom they all knew well. His white, bloodstained shirt was rolled up to his elbows, and his shoulders were bowed in grief. He looked beleaguered and weary. Taking up a stance beside the chair in the corner, the doctor commenced to wring his hands.

Mary's mother, Annabelle, sat beside the bed, her cap askew with strands of tousled gray hair falling around her harried face. A vacant expression registered on her countenance, exhausted from the struggle of dealing with the burden of too much pain. She acknowledged John's presence with a wan smile as tears spilled from eyes already puffy from crying. Oliver, Mary's father, shook his head sorrowfully but maintained his somber watch at his daughter's side.

In the center of the room, Mary lay on a bed graced with a plain iron bedstead. She was groaning and grinding her clenched teeth in agony. White froth mingled with blood was oozing from her pain-distorted mouth.

Anger burned furiously inside of John.

Oh, for some sharp sword of heavenly steel to slay this cruel enemy who is strangling that lovely maiden like an invisible serpent tightening his deadly coils for the kill, he thought.

After a moment, John became aware that the good doctor was now standing at his side. Sorrow dripped from the doctor's words as he said, "Sir, are not God's ways mysterious?"

"God's ways," John said, pointing to the scene of conflict. "How dare you, Dr. Worthington, call that God's way of taking his children home from earth to heaven. No, sir, that is the devil's work."

Righteous indignation flashed from John's eyes like sparks from pieces of flint. "It is time we called on the One who came to destroy the works of the devil, to stop that foul destroyer and save this child."

John turned and faced the doctor. "Can you pray, doctor? Can you pray the prayer of faith that saves the sick?"

John could tell that the doctor was offended at his words.

"You are too much excited, sir," Doctor Worthington said. "'Tis best to say God's will be done." Then he whirled around, grabbed his medical bag, and stormed out of the room.

Excited! John thought. *That word is quite inadequate. Frenzied is more like it…frenzied with Divine anger and hatred of that destroying disease. It is doing Satan's will, not God's.*

When the doctor was gone, John again took note of Mary's diseased-ravaged body twisted into a hideous mass of humanity. Muttering to no one in particular, he said, "It is not so. God would never send such cruelty, and I shall never say God's will be done to Satan's works—the very works that God's own Son came to destroy—this is one of them."

The fresh revelation that was burning in John's heart rose up on the inside and became like a sword—not in his hand, but in his mouth.

"Jesus of Nazareth went about doing good and healing all that were oppressed of the devil, for God was with him. Is not God with us too? Are not all of his promises true?" John looked back and forth from Annabelle to Oliver.

Then resting his hands on the bed, he leaned toward them. "Why did you send for me?"

"We called you to pray." Annabelle wiped her eyes with a handkerchief. "Oh, Pastor, please pray for her that God may raise her up."

John hesitated for just a moment while he turned his focus upward from the conflict raging on the bed to the one who had the power to end all conflicts. Then, out of the intensity of a heart bursting with zeal inspired by the living Word, John lifted up his voice to the redeemer who had stripped the destroyer of his power. "Father, hear our prayer, O Eternal One. Deliver this your child from disease and death. I rest upon the Word. We claim the promise now. The Word is true that says, 'I am the Lord that healeth thee.' Then heal her now."

John began to pace back and forth at the foot of Mary's bed. "Your Word is true. 'I am the Lord, I change not.' Unchanging God, then prove thyself the healer now."

Pounding his fist against the palm of his hand, John continued, "The Word is true. 'These signs shall follow them that believe in my name, they shall lay hands on the sick, and they shall recover.' I believe, and I lay hands on her in Jesus's name and claim this promise now."

John reached over and placed his hand on Mary's burning forehead. "Thy Word is true that says, 'The prayer of faith shall save the sick.' Trusting in thee alone, I cry, oh, save her now. In Jesus's name, amen."

John had hardly gotten the "amen" out of his mouth when Mary ceased thrashing about. Immediately, she fell asleep so soundly that Annabelle asked in a low whisper, "Is she dead?"

"No," John answered. In an even softer whisper, he added, "Mary will live; the fever is gone. She is perfectly well and sleeping as an infant sleeps."

Smoothing the damp hair from Mary's now peaceful brow, John could feel the steady pulsation of her heart and the cool moistness of her hands. Christ had heard his prayer, and just like Jesus had touched Peter's mother-in-law long ago, driving the fever out, Christ the healer had just done the same for Mary.

Excitement filled the room. Annabelle and Oliver embraced each other. Where only moments before there had been tears of grief, now they were replaced with tears of joy.

John's elation knew no bounds. Turning to the nurse who had just entered the room, he said, "Get a cup of cocoa at once and several slices of bread and butter, please."

While Mary slept peacefully, John along with Mary's mother and father sat quietly in awe and reverence, marveling at the power of God while they waited for the nurse to return. When the nourishment arrived, John bent over the bed. Snapping his fingers, he said, "Mary!"

Instantly, she awoke. Smiling sweetly, she noticed John standing beside the bed. "Oh, Pastor, when did you come? I fear I have slept too long."

Then stretching out her arms, she embraced her mother. "Mother, I feel so well." She yawned and then added, "And hungry too."

John poured some cocoa into a saucer and offered it to her. She drank and ate, again and again, until all the bread and drink were gone. After a few minutes, she fell back to sleep, breathing easily and softly.

John tiptoed quietly from her room. Oliver and Annabelle followed, but then led him to the next room where Mary's brother and sister also lay sick with the same fever. John prayed for both of them; they too were instantly healed.

As John left the home, he could not keep from once again singing a song of triumph. Jesus was indeed the same today as he was yesterday.

From that day on, the plague was stayed as far as John's congregation was concerned. Not another person from his flock died of the epidemic.

So the truth that had been entombed in the musty prison house of theology and covered with layers of men's reasoning and Satan's lies had been released once again into the world. As the twentieth century unfolded, so did the knowledge of the truth—never to be buried again. Year after year, the body of Christ grew in power, and little by little all over the globe, the truth succeeded in setting men and women free—delivered from slavery to the wicked ruler of darkness and liberated from the curse that sin had imposed upon mankind.

But God's will was not automatic. It had to be enforced through a believer with the fire of faith in his belly and the Sword of the Spirit in his mouth. When a blood-bought child of God rose up to take dominion on the earth, heavenly hosts raised their swords to destroy the works of the evil one. Satan, who fell like lightning from heaven, had to bow his knee before the new creation who had dominion once again.

Satan's head had been crushed.

Author's End Notes

In 1952, the Lord Jesus Christ appeared to Rev. Kenneth E. Hagin, founder of Rhema Bible Training Center, and talked to him for about an hour and a half about the devil, demons, and demon possession. In this visitation, Brother Hagin learned the same truth in person from the mouth of Jesus Christ that I have endeavored to emphasize in this book through a fictional venue. I would like to share in his words what he relates in his book, *The Believer's Authority*:

> …An evil spirit that looked like a little monkey or elf ran between Jesus and me and spread something like a smoke screen or dark cloud.

> Then this demon began jumping up and down, crying in a shrill voice, "Yakety-yak, yakety-yak, yakety-yak." I couldn't see Jesus or understand what He was saying. . . .

> I couldn't understand why Jesus allowed the demon to make such a racket. I wondered why Jesus didn't rebuke the demon so I could hear what He was saying. I waited a few moments, but Jesus didn't take any action against the demon. Jesus was still talking, but I couldn't understand a word He was saying—and I needed to, because He was giving instructions concerning the devil, demons, and how to exercise authority.

> I thought to myself, *"Doesn't the Lord know I'm not hearing what He wanted me to? I need to hear that. I'm missing it!*

> I almost panicked. I became so desperate I cried out, "In the Name of Jesus, you foul spirit, I command you to stop!"

The minute I said that, the little demon hit the floor like a sack of salt, and the black cloud disappeared. The demon lay there trembling, whimpering, and whining like a whipped pup. He wouldn't look at me. "Not only shut up, but get out of here in Jesus's Name!" I commanded. He ran off.

The Lord knew exactly what was in my mind. I was thinking, *Why didn't He do something about that? Why did He permit it?* Jesus looked at me and said, "If you hadn't done something about that, I couldn't have."

That came as a real shock to me—it astounded me. I replied, "Lord, I know I didn't hear You right! You said You *wouldn't*, didn't You?"

He replied, "No, if you hadn't done something about that, I *couldn't* have."

I went through this four times with Him. He was emphatic about it, saying, "No, I didn't say I *would* not, I said I *could* not."

I said, "Now, dear Lord, I just can't accept that. I never heard or preached anything like that in my life!"

I told the Lord I didn't care how many times I saw Him in visions—He would have to prove this to me by at least three scriptures out of the New Testament (because we're not living under the Old Covenant, we're living under the New). Jesus smiled sweetly and said He would give me four.

I said, "I've read through the New Testament 150 times, and many portions of it more than that. If that is in there, I don't know it!"

Jesus replied, "Son, there is a lot in there you don't know."

He continued, "Not one single time in the New Testament is the Church ever told to pray that God the Father or Jesus would do anything against the devil. In fact, to do so is to waste your time. *The believer* is told to do something about the devil. The reason is because you have the authority to do it. The Church is not to pray to God the Father about the devil; the Church is to exercise the authority that belongs to it.

"The New Testament tells believers themselves to do something about the devil. The least member of the Body of Christ has just as much power over the devil as anyone else, and unless believers do something about the devil, nothing will be done in a lot of areas." . . .

Jesus continued, "I've done all I'm going to do about the devil until the angel comes down from heaven, takes the chain and binds him, and puts him into the bottomless pit" (Rev. 20:1–3 KJV). That came as a real shock to me.

"Now," He said, "I'll give you the four references that prove that. First of all, when I arose from the dead, I said, *'All power* [authority] *is given unto me in heaven and in earth'* (Matt. 28:18 KJV). The word 'power' means 'authority.' But I immediately delegated my authority on earth to the Church, and I can work only *through* the Church, for I am the Head of the Church."

(Your head cannot exercise any authority anywhere except through your body.)

The second reference Jesus gave me was Mark 16:15–18. . . .

He said, "The very first sign mentioned as following *any believer*—not any pastor or any evangelist—is that they shall cast out devils. That means that in my Name they shall exercise authority over the devil, because I have delegated my authority over the devil to the Church." . . .

The next reference Jesus gave me was James 4:7: *"…Resist the devil, and he will flee from you."*…

…My spirit told me the word "flee" was significant. I looked it up in the dictionary and found one of the shades of meanings was "to run from as if in terror." The devil will run from you in terror!

…In the vision Jesus gave me another scripture that tells us to do something about the devil. This third reference was from First Peter. Peter wrote, *"Be sober, be vigilant; because your adversary the devil, as a roaring lion, walketh about, seeking whom he may devour"* (1 Peter 5:8 KJV)….

Jesus said to me in this vision, "Peter did not write the letter and tell Christians, 'Now, word has come to me that God's using our beloved Brother Paul in casting out devils, and he's sending handkerchiefs or cloths, and the diseases are departing from people, and evil spirits are going out of them, so I would suggest that you write to Paul and get a handkerchief.'"

No, instead of that, he told *them* to do something about the devil. Why? Because they've got authority over him….

Ephesians 4:27, *"Neither give place to the devil"* was the fourth scripture Jesus gave to me. He explained, "This means you are not to give the devil any place in you. He cannot take any place unless you give him permission to do so. And you would have to have authority over him or this wouldn't be true."

Jesus added, "Here are your four witnesses. I am the first, James is the second, Peter is the third, and Paul is the fourth. This establishes the fact that the believer has authority on earth, for *I have delegated my authority over the devil to you on the earth.* If you don't do anything about it, nothing will be done. And that is why many times nothing *is* done."

Kenneth E. Hagin, *The Believer's Authority* (Tulsa, OK: Faith Library Publications, 1967, 1986), pp. 35–44. Used with permission. www.rhema.org.)

The book you have just read is not like most other works of fiction because in *Fall Like Lightning from Heaven*, the main character is not a person, but instead a *truth to be revealed.* The knowledge of the believer's authority over Satan is what is often missing in the body of Christ. When I hear stories of disgruntled Christians who have spent years of their lives blaming God for something the devil has done, I realize how vital it is that we rightly discern who is doing what. If we think God is sending accident, calamity, or disease for some mysterious reason that He only has the privilege of knowing, naturally, we have a tendency not to resist.

I do realize that what the devil means for evil can be turned around for good, and many times when the thief comes to steal, kill, and destroy, we do learn valuable lessons about what *not to do* through it all. It is certainly commendable that Christians who have been beleaguered by the relentless attacks of the adversary hang on to their faith and continue to love a God they believe caused or allowed the suffering.

But I believe that the excuse-laden phrase, "Nothing can touch my life unless it is filtered through God's hands first," is propaganda generated by ignorance of the Scriptures. If Satan's head is crushed in your life, it depends on your knowledge of the power that has been invested in you as a believer.

My prayer for you is the same as the one that Paul prayed for the Ephesians.

> [For I always pray to] the God of our Lord Jesus Christ, the Father of glory, that He may grant you a spirit of wisdom and revelation [of insight into mysteries and secrets] in the [deep and intimate] knowledge of Him,
>
> By having the eyes of your heart flooded with light, so that you can know and understand the hope to which He has

called you, and how rich is His glorious inheritance in the saints—His set-apart ones,

And [so that you can know and understand] what is the immeasurable and unlimited and surpassing greatness of His power in and for us who believe, as demonstrated in the working of His mighty strength, which He exerted in Christ when He raised Him from the dead and seated Him at His [own] right hand in the heavenly [places],

Far above all rule and authority and power and dominion and every name that is named [above every title that can be conferred], not only in this age and in this world, but also in the age and the world which are to come.

And He has put all things under His feet and has appointed Him the universal and supreme Head of the church [a headship exercised throughout the church], which is His body, the fullness of Him Who fills all in all [for in that body lives the full measure of Him Who makes everything complete, and Who fills everything everywhere with Himself].

Ephesians 1:17–23

As important as the knowledge of the believer's authority is, in Luke 10:18–20, Jesus lets us know what is even more important. When the disciples returned from a ministry campaign, excited that even the demons were subject to them in his name, Jesus made this statement:

I saw Satan falling like lightning from Heaven. Behold! I have given you authority and power to trample upon serpents and scorpions, and [physical and mental strength and ability] over all the power that the enemy [possesses]; and nothing shall in any way harm you. Nevertheless, do not rejoice at this, that the spirits are subject to you, but rejoice that your names are enrolled in heaven.

Luke 10:18–20

The most important fact you need to know is that your name is written in heaven. If you have not accepted Jesus Christ as your Savior, you have no authority over the devil; in fact, you are still under the *governing* powers of the kingdom of darkness. But I have good news for you: when you make a decision to accept the sacrifice that Jesus made for your sins, you change kingdoms.

Colossians 1:13, 14 says:

> [The Father] has delivered and drawn us to Himself out of the control and the dominion of darkness and has transferred us into the kingdom of the Son of His love, in Whom we have our redemption through His blood, [which means] the forgiveness of our sins.

If you have not accepted Jesus Christ as your Savior but desire to do so, pray this prayer: and then I welcome you into the family of overcomers who are destined *to "reign in life as Kings!"* (Romans 5:17).

> Dear heavenly Father,
>
> I acknowledge I am a sinner and under the dominion of darkness. I accept Jesus Christ as my Lord and Savior and believe that when you raised Him from the dead, all my sins were forgiven. I receive that forgiveness now. I renounce Satan's influence in my life and yield to the Spirit of God to translate me from the kingdom of darkness into the kingdom of light. From this day on, I determine to live my life as a child of God. I am now born again by the Holy Spirit and am a new creature in Christ. My old life has passed away, and I am now ready to begin a new one.
>
> Thank you, Father, that I have a covenant with You because of the blood of Jesus. Satan is under my feet, and he holds no power over me. Make me what You want me to be from now on as I serve You with my whole heart. Amen.

Let us know if you prayed this prayer, and we will send you some information that will help you become established in your walk with God.

Mendenhall Ministries
R.R.3 Box 31 B
Guymon, Oklahoma 73942
mmendenhall.tateauthor.com
E-mail: pastorm@ptsi.net

Afterword

To fictionalize a familiar story of this magnitude requires a great deal of carefulness in order to make it as factual as possible while still expanding it by adding description and dialogue. My desire was to take you, the reader, through the pages of the greatest story ever told and allow you to experience the reality of these well-known scriptural events from a new perspective. To do this, I had to draw information from a variety of sources.

In chapters one through twenty-four, with the exception of chapters four and sixteen, all of the characters are recorded in the Bible except for Rayah, the lion. However, the gospel of Mark 1:12, 13 records, "Immediately the [Holy] Spirit [from within] drove Him out into the wilderness (desert), and He stayed in the wilderness (desert) forty days, being tempted [all the while] by Satan; *and He was with the wild beasts,* and the angels ministered to Him [continually]" (emphasis mine).

We have no record of everything that Jesus went through during those forty days in the wilderness, but we know that the last three temptations were not the only challenges He had to face. Mark says He was tempted all the while; so for forty days, I believe Jesus had to face some of the same ordeals that we also face from our adversary. He had to overcome each test the same way we win the victory over our trials through believing and speaking the Word of God.

Also, Eve's companion, Khawshak, is a fictionalized character; however, we are told that a lamb was slain to cover Adam and Eve after they sinned. I have just given him a name.

The three accounts of Jesus being taught by the Father are taken from the book *Paradise the Holy City and the Glory of the Throne,* written by Rev. Elwood Scott. The author had been approached at the beginning of the twentieth century by an acquaintance,

Seneca Sodi, who related his experience of spending forty days in heaven. He asked Rev. Scott to record this account for him. During his stay in heaven, Mr. Sodi was shown the Book of Life that, among other things, contained records of the Son of God while He was on earth. One of the chapters was entitled "Jesus Taught by the Father." While Rev. Scott's book does not relate all of the details surrounding these three events, the information I have included in *Fall Like Lightning from Heaven* is consistent with the information from that book in regard to the messages given and locations as to where they occurred.

The descriptions of heaven, hell, angels, and Satan all come from a wealth of books written by eye witnesses who have had real experiences of visiting heaven and hell, in addition to those who have had encounters with demons and heavenly beings.

The chapters taking place in Sydney, Australia, are a fictionalized account of true events that took place in the life of John Alexander Dowie that happened at the end of the nineteenth century.

Even though *Fall Like Lightning from Heaven* is categorized as fiction, the message it delivers is true. Many times, we recount the events pertaining to our salvation void of feeling. Often, we unconsciously place very little value on all that Jesus went through to purchase our redemption and regain the authority that we now have the privilege of enjoying. I have tried to remedy that by presenting the time-honored information from the Scriptures in a way designed to appeal to all the senses, thus, making the story of redemption come alive for the reader.

Some might think it is not right for an author to presume to know what was going through the mind of Jesus or even add to the Scriptures in any way through such a story as this. However, 1 Corinthians 2: 13, 16 says,

> And we are setting these truths forth in words not taught by human wisdom but taught by the [Holy] Spirit, combining and interpreting spiritual truths with spiritual lan-

guage [to those who possess the Holy Spirit]. For who has known or understood the mind (the counsels and purposes) of the Lord so as to guide and instruct Him and give Him knowledge? *But we have the mind of Christ* (the Messiah) *and do hold the thoughts* (feelings and purposes) *of His heart.* (emphasis mine)

As we approach the end of this age, I believe the Holy Spirit is using every means possible to reveal to mankind the power of God that is available to the believer and the loving heart of the Father who yearns to see His creation set free from the ravages of Satan. That is the purpose of this book. As you have walked through the Scriptures and agonized with the characters, it is my prayer that you will rise up in Jesus's name against the enemy in your life and that you will confidently enforce what Satan experienced when he fell like lightning from heaven, and in the process, become empowered to crush him under your feet.

Lexicon of Scriptures Referred to in the Text

Since the events recorded in this book are primarily based on the Scriptures, included is a list of verses I have referred to. You can use this list as a convenient guide to help you study the Bible as you read *Fall Like Lightning from Heaven* or use it as a handy reference to check the accuracy of the facts.

Prologue:
    A fictionalized account of a true event in the life of John Alexander Dowie taken from the book *John Alexander Dowie* by Gordon Lindsay; published by Christ for the Nations, Dallas, Texas; 1980.

Chapter One:
    Genesis 1:26-28
    Genesis 3:1-15
    James 1:14 & 15
    Proverbs 7:23
    1 John 4:18 (Amplified Bible)
    Revelation 19:12 & 15

Chapter Two:
    Genesis 3:16-24
    Revelations 1:13-16
    Ezekiel 18:4
    Isaiah 53:7
    John 15:13
    Psalms 32:1

Chapter Three:
    Genesis 6:5 & 6
    Revelation 12:7-9
    Isaiah 14:12-15
    Ezekiel 28:12-17
    Luke 10:18
    Psalms 8:4-9
    1 John 5:19
    Ephesians 6:12
    Matthew 2:16-18
    Matthew 3:17

Chapter Five:
    Mark 1:12 & 13
    Matthew 4:1
    Luke 4:1
    Psalms 118:24
    Mark 1:5-8
    Matthew 3:15
    John 1:26-36
    Daniel 6:16-22

Chapter Six:
    Psalms 40:8
    Luke 2:41-52

Chapter Seven:
    Psalms 19:1
    Psalms 21:3 & 6
    Revelation 21:11-14 & 18-23
    Revelation 7:12
    Revelation 5:13

Chapter Eight:
  Revelation 13:8
  Ezekiel 28:12-15
  Luke 10:18
  Hebrews 9:14

Chapter Nine:
  Romans 5:12
  Hebrews 10:1, 3, 4, 5, 7 & 20
  Hebrews 9:14
  Isaiah 53:3-5
  Romans 5:17
  Matthew 16:18
  1 Corinthians 15:54-57
  1 John 3:8
  Hebrews 12:2

Chapter Ten:
  Matthew 9:36
  1 Peter 5:8
  Psalms 91
  Luke 10:19
  Acts 13:10
  James 4:7
  Hebrews 4:15

Chapter Eleven:
  John 8:14-18
  John 12:49
  John 8:44
  Psalms 57:1
  Mark 8:33
  Psalms 57:2
  Mark 4:39

Psalms 29:11
Psalms 55:18
Psalms 30:11 & 12
Psalms 18:29
1 John 4:4

Chapter Twelve:
Matthew 4:4
Psalms 91:11
Isaiah 53:4 & 5
Matthew. 4:7

Chapter Thirteen:
James 2:17
2 Corinthians 11:14
Luke 4:6-8
Matthew 16:26
Hebrews 4:12
Luke 4:13

Chapter Fourteen:
Psalms 20:6
Psalms 18:30
Psalms 18:2
Psalms 40:2, 3, & 8
Luke 22:31 & 32
2 Corinthians 5:7
Hebrews 4:15
1 John 2:16
Hebrews 2:18
Luke 4:18
Isaiah 61:1
Matthew 10:8
Matthew 4:16

Chapter Fifteen:
    Luke 4:16-41
    Matthew 8:14 & 15
    Matthew 4:23
    Matthew 9: 35
    Mark 5:1-20
    Matthew 8:8
    Luke 6:27 & 28
    Romans 12:14
    Romans 12:17-21
    John 11:1-44

Chapter Seventeen:
    Luke 19:46
    Matthew 21:12 & 13
    Mark 11:15 & 16
    Luke 13:33 & 34
    Matthew 26:17 & 18
    Mark 14:15
    Luke 22:12
    John 13:1-17
    Matthew 20:25-26
    Psalms 41:9
    John 13:18
    Matthew 26:21
    John 13:26

Chapter Eighteen:
    Luke 22:19 & 20
    1 Corinthians 11:25
    John 6:35-69
    John 13:31-38
    Luke 22:31 & 32
    John 14

John 16:24-33
John 17

Chapter Nineteen:
Matthew 26:37-44
Mark 14:32-40
Luke 22:39-46
2 Corinthians 5:21
Leviticus 16:8-10

Chapter Twenty:
Matthew 26:45-56
Mark 14:41-50
Luke 22:47-53

Chapter Twenty-One:
Matthew 26:57-27:31
Mark 14:53-15:22
Luke 22:54-23:25
Psalm 118:24
Ephesians 3:16
Psalms 22:11
Isaiah 53:5

Chapter Twenty-Two:
Matthew 27:32-54
Mark 15:21-39
Luke 23:26-47
John 19:16-30
Isaiah 53:4
Hebrews 10:19 & 20
Hebrews 4:16

Chapter Twenty-Three:
Isaiah 1:18
Romans 5:18
Revelation 1:18
Romans 5:17
Colossians 1:18
Revelation 1:5
Matthew 12:40

Chapter Twenty-Four:
John 20
Matthew 28
Mark 16
Luke 24
Matthew 16:19
Mark 16:15-19
1 John 4:4
John 17:10,13,15,17,18,20, & 24
Colossians 1:13
Matthew 16:18
2 Corinthians 5:17 & 21
Romans 5:17

Chapter Twenty-Five:
Acts 2:2-4
Acts 2:41
Acts 5:15
Acts 8:1-3
Acts 9
1 Corinthians 2:8
Ephesians 1:17-23

Chapter Twenty-Six:
    Acts 10:38
    Hebrews 13:8
    James 5:14 & 15
    1 John 3:8
    Exodus 15:26
    Malachi 3:6
    Mark 16:17 & 18
    Luke 10:18
    Genesis 3:15

Bibliography

Paradise the Holy City and the Glory of the Throne, by Rev. Elwood Scott. Engeltal Press, P.O. Box. 447, Jasper, ARK 72641, 1984.

John Alexander Dowie, by Gordon Lindsay. Christ for the Nations, Inc. Dallas, Texas, 1980.

Angels on Assignment, by Roland Buck as told to Charles & Frances Hunter, Hunter Books, 1602 Townhurst, Houston, Texas 77043, 1979.

Heaven, Close Encounters of the God Kind, by Dr. Jesse Duplantis, Jesse Duplantis Ministries, PO Box 20149, New Orleans, Louisiana 70141, 1996.

A Divine Revelation of the Spirit Realm, by Mary Baxter with Dr. T. L. Lowery, Whitaker House, 30 Hunt Valley Circle, New Kensington, PA 15068, 2000.

Snatched from Satan's Claws, by Kaniaki, D.D and Mukendi, Enkei Media Services Ltd., Nairobi, Kenya, 1991.

The Believer's Authority, by Kenneth E. Hagin, (Tulsa, OK: Faith Library Publications, 1967, 1986), pp. 35-44. Used with permission. www.rhema.org.

23 Minutes in Hell, by Bill Wiese, Charisma House, A Strang Company, 600 Rinehart Road, Lake Mary, Florida 32746, 2006.

Contact Information

For speaking engagements or comments contact:
Margaret Mendenhall
Victory Center Church
P. O. Box 128
Guymon, OK, 73942
E-Mail pastorm@ptsi.net
Phone 580-338-5616

listen|imagine|view|experience

AUDIO BOOK DOWNLOAD INCLUDED WITH THIS BOOK!

In your hands you hold a complete digital entertainment package. In addition to the paper version, you receive a free download of the audio version of this book. Simply use the code listed below when visiting our website. Once downloaded to your computer, you can listen to the book through your computer's speakers, burn it to an audio CD or save the file to your portable music device (such as Apple's popular iPod) and listen on the go!

How to get your free audio book digital download:

1. Visit www.tatepublishing.com and click on the e|LIVE logo on the home page.
2. Enter the following coupon code:
   398d-5704-8449-0e61-92cc-7efb-2bd4-2102
3. Download the audio book from your e|LIVE digital locker and begin enjoying your new digital entertainment package today!